A Pride & Prejudice
Time Travel Romance

# Moments of Moments Present

THE MEMORY SERIES #2

# NEY MITCH

*Good day, Reader, if you are back, that means that you enjoyed the first installment, therefore I hope you enjoy this second one.*
*Therefore, this one is once more dedicated to you for returning to the world of the series and following these characters to whatever end. You all are wonderful!*

# Chapter One

## DISAPPOINTMENT

I n faith, what an insufferably rude man! As we drove in our carriage away from the Assembly Room for the evening, Jane was quite excited from her happy spirits, Lydia and Kitty were voluble as usual, Mary did not speak, but only looked out of the window, my mother was roused, full of excitement as she kept congratulating Jane on her triumph for the evening, and I was left to my own thoughts.

Looking out of the carriage window, I glimpsed the scenery as we passed it by, and it allowed my mind to wonder about the scene that we had just left when the assembly dance had come to an end…

When the Netherfield party had entered, rumors turned out to have been greatly exaggerated. Some people reported that twenty would come, some that it was ten, others that it would be seven, but in the end, there were only five of them altogether. There was Mr. Charles Bingley, with his two sisters; the first was Mrs. Louisa Hurst, who came with her husband, Mr. Hurst, who looked bored, tedious, out of sorts and overall dour.

The other sister was the largest shock and she scared me tremendously, for her name was Caroline Bingley. Yet even before I knew her name, the resemblance between her and her future self were quite remarkable, so I had no choice but to flinch when seeing her. Yet when I heard her name uttered, I could not have been more flabbergasted. Thank goodness that I was told who she was rather than her making my acquaintance and then awkwardness ensuing afterwards. No, I was only left to marvel at the coincidence, feel great pain over it, and having no other choice but to immediately develop a prejudice toward her.

Yet when Sir William had presented Mr. Bingley to our company, Mr. Darcy had no choice but to follow behind his friend. My eagerness to see him had clouded my judgment. I was happy and clearly had no choice but to be so.

"Mrs. Bennet," Sir William said, "Mr. Bingley has expressly desired to become acquainted with you and your daughters."

"Oh, we are glad to hear it," our mother had replied, and then she introduced us all individually. While Mr. Bingley had been asking Jane if she would like to dance, I had taken the opportunity to test Mr. Darcy, to see if he was the same man that I had fallen in love with in 2016. But when he failed it, not understanding the reference I gave, I lost all hope of him being the same person. That Mr. Darcy, of the 21$^{st}$ century, was now lost to me. Yet this one was present, and therefore I would do the best I could to warm myself to him and at least find comfort in his presence.

Yet that goal, that very aim, came to an immediate and quick halt very soon.

After Mr. Bingley had requested my sister's hand, she had said yes, and they were to dance the next set together. Yet I, standing there and with no offers for a partner, drew the empathy of my mother. Seeing Mr. Darcy standing there and making no offer, she looked at me and then at Mr. Darcy.

She smiled at him. "And you, sir, you are also very welcome to Hertfordshire, as is with your pleasant and amiable friend."

"Thank you, ma'am," Mr. Darcy replied, but his voice and tone held no warmth.

"I hope that you find yourself most amenable to the activity of dancing as well, as your friend here."

"I rarely dance," Mr. Darcy replied simply. "It is not my favorite activity."

"Oh, many a man has said such a thing before he goes to the dance floor, and then quickly forgets once he is there and becomes all smiles! Let our humble assembly help you to forget that, for here," and here she turned to me, "we have many lovely choices for partners."

Yet this gentle hint for him to ask me clearly was too much for Mr. Darcy's *sensibilities*, for he quickly bowed his head, excused himself and walked away to remain next to Caroline Bingley and Mrs. Hurst.

He had slighted me!

And once more, he flocked to Caroline Bingley.

Indeed, I didn't know which aspect to be more offended by. Yet, as he did so, I refused to look upset or affected. Luckily, for my part, I did not need to; for Mr. Bingley noticed and noted his friend's coldness, because he then went on to ask me if he could dance with me in the next set. I happily agreed, and then he excused himself to tend to his friend.

Once both men had left our company, my mother was ready to release all her rage at what had just transpired.

"Well, what an odious and hateful man!" she exclaimed. "Who is he to raise his nose up to anyone and be so disobliging!"

"Mama," I magnified, "thank you so very much, but you must not speak so very loudly, or you shall be overheard."

"Then let me be so," she countered. "I would be perfectly willing to have all of Hertfordshire hear me, for that was outrageous. And his friend is so willing to be charming, making the perfect picture of a gentleman, except for that blot of ink that is his horrid friend."

While I worried about her voice carrying and being overheard, I do not deny that I was secretly flattered by her willingness to come to my defense. Such a desire to protect me was keenly felt and I did feel a certain amount of warmth for it. While I knew very well that she would protect any of us sisters equally, I still felt special in that moment and I warmed to it.

Yet therein lay the matter of Mr. Darcy himself.

Such an introduction naturally did not live up to my expectations, and therefore while I sat down for a dance, due to a lack of a partner, my mind could not help but reflect on our disastrous first meeting.

At first, I had wished to give him a bit of a set down, and then that desire was quickly overcome and an intense desire to see my first Mr. Darcy again had rested in its proper place. Until I recalled that my first meeting with Mr. Fitzwilliam Darcy in 2016 did not go very well initially, and I had actually developed a dislike for him originally.

Only a shared experience of us falling back through time had united us and helped us reach an understanding and connection. Yet initially, our acquaintance had begun in a strained fashion. Therefore, while Mr. Darcy had slighted me, there was always room for improvement, for changed opinions, and maybe, as I had learned very easily, time could improve our situation.

Yet the circumstance proved to have been quite different, and my disdain for *this present* Mr. Darcy had quickly been cemented by his continual behavior and disposition throughout the evening.

The two new men in our presence had painted their own individual portraits quite well, and each in extreme contrast to the other. Mr. Bingley was good-looking and gentlemanlike. He had a pleasant countenance, and easy, unaffected manners. Mr. Darcy soon drew the attention of the room by his fine, tall person, handsome features, noble mien, and the report which was in general circulation since his stepping foot into Hertfordshire, of his having ten thousand a year.

The gentlemen pronounced him to be a fine figure of a man, the ladies declared he was much handsomer than Mr. Bingley, and he was looked at with great admiration for about half the evening, till his manners gave a disgust which turned the tide of his popularity.

Mr. Darcy would prove that money and fortune could not always buy popular or good opinion, for he presented in full what he had shown me when we first met. Very quickly, he was discovered to be proud, to be above his company, and above being pleased, and not all his large estate in Derbyshire could then save him from having a most forbidding, disagreeable countenance, and being unworthy to be compared with his friend.

Mr. Bingley was likable and very quickly made himself liked by all in the assembly room, while Mr. Darcy made himself the most hated. Mr. Bingley had soon made himself acquainted with all the principal people in the room. He was lively and unreserved, danced every dance, was upset that the ball closed so early, and talked of giving one himself at Netherfield. Such amiable qualities must speak for themselves. What a contrast between him and his friend! Mr. Darcy danced only once with Mrs. Hurst and once with Miss Bingley, declined being introduced to any other lady, and spent the rest of the evening in walking about the room, speaking occasionally to one of his own party.

"He is the proudest, most disagreeable man in the world," Kitty whispered to me as she was near me, taking some punch in between dances. "And everybody hopes that he would never come here again. Literally, Lizzy, he stood by me for three whole minutes a little time ago, and he didn't speak to me once. He didn't even ask me to dance! And it's a new rule that I set down, that if a man does not offer to dance with me after three minutes of standing next to me at an assembly, then that must mean that he is the worst man in England!"

"I would say that is an extreme reaction, Kitty," I remarked, "but in this matter, I know how you feel."

Yet the largest offense of the evening of this 'Mr. Darcy' to me would not have come until the latter of the evening. I had been obliged, by the scarcity of gentlemen, to sit down for two dances. While I remained there, Mr. Darcy had found himself to be standing near me for quite some time.

Yet did he ask me to dance?

No, he did not.

Did he speak to me at all?

By no means.

Did he at least look upon me?

Not at all.

The other Mr. Darcy, the proper one, would have at least noted me.

Yet this willful ignorance was enhanced and eclipsed when Mr. Bingley, all smiles and cheeriness from coming back and dancing with Jane, accosted his taciturn friend.

"Come, Darcy," he implored. "I must have you dance. I hate to see you standing about by yourself in this stupid manner. You had much better dance."

"I certainly shall not," Mr. Darcy replied. "You know how I detest it, unless I am particularly acquainted with my partner. At such an assembly as this it would be insupportable. Your sisters are engaged, and there is not another woman in the room whom it would not be a punishment to me to stand up with."

That was the first full set of sentences that I had heard him speak, and each sentence was less charming than the next.

"I would not be so fastidious as you are," cried Mr. Bingley, "for a kingdom! Upon my honor, I never met with so many pleasant girls in my life as I have this evening, and there are several of them you see uncommonly pretty."

Here, Mr. Bingley's eyes scanned over the crowd and he cast his amiable and admiring eye on my sister. Such a sight made me feel a slight bit of warmth, because, as you may recall, before my interesting adventure in the future, I had predicted that if there was one of us Bennet sisters who could possibly draw the affection of Mr. Bingley, it would be Jane, therefore I was content in that I was correct. And Jane, well, she had quite deserved Mr. Bingley's admiration, if that was what he had felt for her.

When I looked back at the two men once more, they still had not observed me sitting so close to them, so they continued on, in the artless and honest discussion that men give when they do not expect to be overheard by any surrounding observers.

"*You* are dancing with the only handsome girl in the room," said Mr. Darcy, looking at Jane as well. While I at first was happy that he noticed my sister's superior beauty, I very quickly grew vexed that his statement implied that I was not worthy for anyone's consideration, especially his own. He might as well had called me inadequate.

"Oh!" Mr. Bingley replied. "She is the most beautiful creature I ever beheld! But there is one of her sisters sitting down just behind you, who is very pretty, and I dare say very agreeable. Do let me ask Miss Bennet to have you presented to her, and then you can stand up with her."

"Which do you mean?"

Mr. Darcy therefore turned around just in time for me to look away and pretend as if I had been quite oblivious to their discussion. Yet out of the corner of my eye, I still saw him look on me, squint meanly and then look away as quickly as he could.

"She is tolerable, but not handsome enough to tempt *me*."

Such a cold thing to say! Such a terribly cold thing!

"I am in no humor at present to give consequence to young ladies who are slighted by other men. You had better return to your partner and enjoy her smiles, for you are wasting your time with me."

Mr. Bingley, who seemed used to his friend's disposition, had quite given up, and left his friend to wallow in his own wretchedness, standing there, like the statue that he was. Indeed, he was quite made of marble, in that he was like stone and seemed to draw no warmth or natural feeling of any kind.

Such harshness, some meanness, only to be made even more extreme against my memory of the first Mr. Darcy I had become acquainted with. When I had told him that compared to Jane, I was not so admired, and he denied this, stating the reverse and that while he believed my statements of her perfection, I would not and should not ever consider myself second best. He believed in me! And when I had asked him to dance, he had danced with me!

How quickly his ancestor, this Mr. Darcy, did not live up to the other's shadow. How ironic that the shade of the descendant had quite eclipsed his great—great—great—great ancestor's height. This Mr. Darcy was not even half the man who would spring from his line, and that made him such a...

"Bumface!" I accidentally said aloud, and while it was not too much in volume, it was just enough for Mr. Darcy to have heard me and therefore to turn his head. Then he noticed me once more, and in his eyes was a feeling of distaste. I think it then began to occur to him that just maybe I did overhear everything that he had said.

"I beg your pardon? What did you say?"

I bit my lip, wondering what ought to be done. I had been overheard and I had, for a brief moment, lost all sense of self control. Yet then again, I did not desire to be so self-contained. My dip into the future had quite altered me in some respects, as it would have, and I did not feel the need to conceal all and suffer long under the weight of miscommunication and comedies of errors. Therefore, I had the impulse, and as much as it would counteract my initial intention, I stood up and stared him square in the face.

I gave him a cool smile. "Bumface, sir. I said bumface."

He gave me a quizzical look. "Pray tell me, what does that mean?"

"I am certain, sir, with your prestigious heritage, that you have been given some of the best of education."

"I believe that I have."

"Well, you therefore must have developed deductive reasoning. What does it mean, you ask? I trust, sir, that in time, you shall figure it out."

With that, I curtsied to him and thus walked away.

As I did so, I saw Charlotte standing in a corner and she nodded to me, smiled, waved and clearly expected me to come over to her. I smiled, gestured that I had to go to my family, and she looked slightly disappointed before she turned to her sister, Maria, and conversed with her.

I so much wished to speak with her sometimes, but since I had returned from my adventure in time, I had visited her scarcely, and when she had come to Longbourn to see me, I was kind, but never warm.

I knew Charlotte, and she clearly would have noticed the difference, the very change in my disposition. I missed her a great deal, but time had given me too much foreknowledge, and now I saw the dangers of it. Every time that I had seen her, I now knew that she would be the woman to marry my cousin and assist in my family being driven from Longbourn. I suppose that I could not forgive her for a future that she hadn't even lived yet.

I hoped that such distrust and unease would dissolve very quickly, yet I could not help but take it all to heart, and to head. Therefore, I walked to the table, got myself some punch, drank it, and then I left the assembly room to get some time alone in the hall, where I knew no one would follow me.

That was how the evening had transpired. With me being greatly offended by a man who did all in his power to make himself the most despised man to enter Hertfordshire.

I remained with no very cordial feelings toward him. Yet, though I did not tell Charlotte, I unfolded the story to Jane and Kitty, for despite Mr. Darcy being a substantial disappointment, my lively, playful disposition, which delighted in anything ridiculous, would not miss the opportunity to speak about it.

We drove along toward home still, and as I looked at my family, feeling the bumpiness of the road, I could not resist as I mumbled to myself.

"I miss buses and cars. So much more convenient."

# Chapter Two

## THE RIFT

When we returned to Longbourn at last, our father was waiting for us in the sitting room, ready to expect a full report from our mother, and he was sure to get it.

She reported about how the evening altogether passed off pleasantly to the whole family while we all sat down, and tea was brought out for us.

"Jane was so much admired by our new neighbors! And it was most pleasant. The Netherfield Party adored everything about her. Mr. Bingley had danced with her twice, and she had been distinguished by his sisters."

I looked toward Jane, smiled at her, and while she was delighted by this, as always, she did it in a much quieter way. Yet still, I welcomed Jane's pleasure and patted her leg.

"Good job on your triumph," I whispered.

"Oh, Lizzy, I have triumphed over nothing."

"You have," I urged her to believe, "and you know it. Revel in it, dear Jane, for you deserve it."

Jane smiled, blushed and looked down.

"And Mary was mentioned to Miss Bingley as the most accomplished girl in the neighborhood," my mother continued, which was nice, for Mary rarely ever got complimented, so this swelled her pride for the moment. "And Catherine and Lydia had been fortunate enough never to be without partners."

"And that is all that we had yet learnt to care for at a ball," Lydia cried.

"Therefore, we return home in good spirits," Kitty said. "But I find that I still have it within me to dance one more dance."

"As do I," Lydia said, then she took Kitty's hands, pulled her up and they began to dance around the room.

"Oh! My dear Mr. Bennet," our mother continued. "We really did have a most delightful evening, a most excellent ball. I wish you had been there. Jane's good fortune was so marked, nothing could be like it. Mr. Bingley thought her quite beautiful and danced with her twice! Only think of *that*, my dear, he actually danced with her twice! And she was the only creature in the room that he asked a second time."

She made a moue. "First of all, he asked Miss Lucas. I was so vexed to see him stand up with her! But, however, he did not admire her at all, indeed, nobody can, you know, and he seemed quite struck with Jane as she was going down the dance. So, he inquired who she was, and got introduced, and asked her for the two next. Then the two third he danced with Miss King, and the two fourth with Maria Lucas, and the two fifth with Jane again, and the two sixth with Lizzy, and the *Boulanger*—"

"If he had had any compassion for *me*," our father declared, clearly disappointed that our mother was not let down by Mr. Bingley at all, "he would not have danced half so much! For God's sake, say no more of his partners. Oh, that he had sprained his ankle in the first dance."

I knew my father, and since our expectations had been raised to such a degree for this ball, he quite hoped that we would find something wanting in Mr. Bingley. But it was not to be so.

My mother then began to praise Mr. Bingley more, remarking on how charming he was, on how elegant his sisters were and here I flinched, for to hear any incarnation of Miss Bingley be regarded as such was like ringing in my ears. And then my mother turned her report toward another branch of subject, of the insufferably rude Mr. Darcy.

"The foolish and odious man slighted poor Lizzy," she added, "and refused to be obliging and stand up with her."

"He slighted my dear Lizzy?" My father raised an eyebrow.

"Father, you need not worry," I assured him, "for between his rude manner and very tedious voice, I suppose I lose nothing, for if he liked me, then I would have to actually talk to him."

"And I assure you," my mother pressed, "that you do not lose much by not suiting *his* fancy. For he is a most disagreeable, horrid man, not at all worth pleasing. So high and so conceited that there was no enduring him! He walked here, and he walked there, fancying himself so very great! Not handsome enough to dance with! I wish you had been there, my dear, to have given him one of your set-downs. I quite detest the man."

"You are at liberty to do so," my father replied, actually a little sincere, "for he knows not the value of anything."

I looked at my father and could not believe his staunch support of me in that moment. Yes, he favored me, but now it was so sincere and marked that it was quite surprising.

"Thank you, Father."

"Yes, well." He sat down once more and opened his book. "Always remember, he may prefer a stupid wife, as others have done before him. The good taste of men, like that of women often, is entirely a matter of chance. Therefore, offense ought never to be taken for when we turn up our noses at you. For to be a man, is at some point, to walk past every woman who you should have found worthy, then approach the one woman who was not worthy at all and think she was the ideal. We humans are quite ironic in that way."

I gave him a warm smile. "I suppose I shall have to be content with that, for I love a good argument, but irony is a force that even I cannot fight."

"No one can, my dear, no one can."

Out of the corner of my eye, I saw my mother and she looked so very thoroughly confused, for I did believe that the conversation had taken a turn in a direction that she did not understand. So, she continued to speak about Mr. Darcy, and how he was the worst man in all of England.

While to the outside observer, this judgment could be regarded as harsh, from my viewpoint within, it satisfied me greatly and felt thoroughly justified.

I had known the best man in all of England once before, and when having such a model in my memory, it could not be undone. And yet, did it follow that I ought to forsake this Mr. Darcy, especially since I promised his descendant so very faithfully that I would look after his ancestor and discover what could possibly happen to him? Therefore, what was I to do? Was I to give into the prejudice that was quickly rising within me, or consider attempting to improve our relationship?

Yet neither decision mattered if Mr. Darcy would not let me in. If he would continue to despise me, then all my deliberations would not have mattered in the end. One cannot forge a link to something that wished for no bonds, and that dismissed you so very soon.

Yes, I wished to resent him.

Yet I had promised Mr. Darcy in 2016... I had made a promise. Therefore, I ought to try and forgive *this* Mr. Darcy, despite every voice in me wishing to give way to implacable resentment.

But only if this Mr. Darcy would one day let me.

☙❧

The next day arrived, and we still were speaking about the assembly. Yet when the conversation turned to Mr. Darcy, we were interrupted, for at the gate of Longbourn, Charlotte Lucas, along with her sister, Maria, had come to visit us and were present. This ought to have not surprised me. For after a ball of any sort, for friends to all visit one and speak of it seems to always be a rule. But I had been out of time and place for so very long, that I was quite out of touch with many things, including being of good spirits and being able to welcome Charlotte.

There she was, waving to me merrily, and I could not separate from my mind the truth about her future. Therefore, as I accosted her, I did not run or eagerly go to meet her but approached her with care and consideration. In her eyes, I saw the marked difference. Between my not visiting or caring to see her since I had come back to Longbourn from the future, to my not seeking her out at the assembly room, to my lack of spirits now, I did believe that she was soon growing to notice that something was amiss.

However, it was so very difficult, for as I looked into her face, I just could not help but always think the same thing:

'You will marry my cousin and leave my family homeless. Without a care or a second thought.'

This mindset was ungenerous, I do not deny, for I had not known the full story. After all, I had never met Mr. Collins before, so there was always the possibility that he was handsome and she would fall in love with him, or that she felt so very much pressured to agree for some reason or another, but then there was the other possibility, and that was that she was truly doing it only for herself and her situation, as Mr. Darcy had pointed out when we discovered it.

"Lizzy." Charlotte smiled, forcefully, and I could tell that she understood that there was something different between us and it was strained. Knowing that I had to do my best to conceal this as much as I could, I therefore decided that it was best to fake a comfort that I did not feel.

"My dear Charlotte," I cried, putting more life in my step. "And Maria, come to see us then?"

Maria gave a merry laugh. "Yes, we do. We have much to talk about."

"As one ought to after a ball," I added, "for if one does not repeat what are the goings on were, then a ball was not proper, now was it?"

I turned to Charlotte and smiled.

"We did not get the chance to talk much at the ball," I acknowledged.

"No," she confirmed, "no we did not. Yet, I am here now, and therefore we had best make up for the time you have spent ill."

"Ill?" Maria asked. "Were you ill, Lizzy?"

"Oh, well I…"

"Of course, she was a little indisposed," Charlotte answered for me, "for she has remained in Longbourn in seclusion for over a week. And we know that Elizabeth never does such a thing."

I looked to Charlotte and I realized that she was telling herself what she wanted to hear, due to the fact that she needed something to believe other than me avoiding her. I knew that it would help her as well, and also help me, but I knew that I would need a greater excuse, in case my discomfort around her lasted a little longer than I desired. I wanted to get over this distrust of her, but one cannot forget things so easily, nor always be governed over by logic rather than emotion and our passions. I wanted to get over it quickly, but I couldn't.

"Oh, Charlotte," I said, "forgive me, while I have not necessarily been ill, I have been indisposed, but only in the sense that I have been undertaking an activity that requires me to take many moments to myself, in order for improvement."

"Improvement? Goodness, what is this new activity that has taken you away from me?"

"Oh, well, forgive me, but I cannot tell you at present," I answered, stalling. "Yet never fear, Charlotte, when I feel that I have improved enough that I am ready for others to know of it, then you shall be the first that I tell. And be not offended for my secrecy, for even Jane here does not know of it."

Jane looked at me strangely, but then she confirmed this. Charlotte smiled diplomatically, but I knew her mind, and the fact was that she always felt that I told her everything.

And now I wasn't.

And she must never know why.

"*You* began the evening well, Charlotte," our mother said when Charlotte, Maria, Jane and I sat down in the parlor. "*You* were Mr. Bingley's first choice."

"Yes," Charlotte replied, then she smiled at Jane, and was very diplomatic to our mother. "But he seemed to like his second better."

This was enough to put our mother on a speech about how well Jane did for the evening.

"Oh! You mean Jane, I suppose, because he danced with her twice."

They continued to talk on about how Mr. Bingley had told our neighbor, Mr. Robinson, about how he thought Jane was the loveliest woman that he had ever seen, dancing around the idea of Jane being ideal for Mr. Bingley, when my mother turned the subject to me.

"*Your* over-hearings were more to the purpose than *Lizzy's*, Charlotte," our mother stressed, then she turned to me. "Mr. Darcy is not so well worth listening to as his friend, is he? My poor Eliza! To be only just *tolerable*."

"I do not understand," Charlotte replied, looking between my mother and me. "Was it something that I have quite forgotten?"

"Oh," I rushed out, "forgive me, Charlotte, in the excitement of the evening, I forgot to inform you."

Startled, my mother asked, "You didn't tell Charlotte? Oh, I never would have thought it. Did you not wish to speak of it, Lizzy? For I can assure you that you need not be ashamed by it."

"I am not ashamed, I assure you, mother," I pointed out, and I very much wished to kick her for her continuous talk and inability to take a hint. "I merely never got the chance to unfold the story to Charlotte and Maria here, but now that they are come, I can unfold all."

I turned to Charlotte and Maria, then told them about what had transpired for the evening before. When I had finished, Maria was the more vocal of the two.

"Oh, poor Lizzy!" she cried. "It was very mean of him to speak so."

"Yes, it was," I replied, smiling. "A capital offense."

"Well," Charlotte added after being silent for a time. "As your mother said, he is not worthy of your concern, and his ten thousand pounds a year perhaps is not even enough to make up for a lackluster disposition. No, for even those are too costly on a woman's sanity."

I laughed at this. "Precisely. And as a result, I would not care for him, unless his personality begins to match the sum of his income, but it would take a biblical miracle to make such a change."

"Oh, and he really called you 'just tolerable'?"

"I beg you would not put it into Lizzy's head to be vexed by his ill-treatment," our mother stressed, "for he is such a disagreeable man, that it would be quite a misfortune to be liked by him."

"Miss Bingley told me," Jane said, "that he never speaks much, unless among his intimate acquaintances. With *them* he is remarkably agreeable."

"Jane," I whispered. "Must you defend the man who has offended me so very a short time ago?"

"Oh yes, I forgot," she whispered on reply, "Sorry."

"I do not believe a word of it, my dear," our mother replied, willing to hate the man who slighted me forever.

"He should have danced with you, Lizzy," Charlotte answered, warmly.

"Thank you, Charlotte," I said. "While I care little, I do wish that at least he had gathered the kindness to have done that."

"Another time, Lizzy," my mother pressed, "I would not dance with *him*, if I were you."

At first, I was to reply in that I would never dance with him, and the side of me that was very much desiring to despise him for not living up to any dream that I had of him was willing to do so. Yet time had taught me, and also had anchored me down to the possibility that even he could improve upon closer acquaintance. Therefore, rather than be severe, I was instead willing to be diplomatic.

"I believe, ma'am," I concluded, "that if he continues on this path, of being such an insufferable man, then I may safely promise you *never* to dance with Mr. Darcy. Yet if he improves, learns the error of his mindset and seeks to make amends, I shall consider dancing with him… but only if I know in advance if he is the best dancer in all of Derbyshire."

All in our company laughed, and while I did so, there was a quick flash in my mind of when Mr. Darcy and I danced at Pemberly, and he had struggled to learn the steps, but even then there was greatness to every movement of his.

Thus, I wondered what he was doing in his own time, while I was back within mine. Safe and sound, but not secure. For I was quite torn. A part of me was here, but another part of me was somewhere else, always there, with him. And I worried, for indeed, how long was my soul going to be divided?

Eventually Charlotte and Maria's visit came to an end, and while the sisters were leaving, Jane and I escorted them out.

"I can see why you did not wish to speak of it at first, Elizabeth," Charlotte whispered to me. "For I know that such a slight is sometimes hard to hear and feel."

"Yes," was all that I could say.

"But truly, we have been friends too long for you to feel any sort of shame. You know not only would nothing dampen my opinion of you, but also that I shall always be by your side."

*Until you are not. Until the day that you don't care about our friendship at all.*

"Yes, I did not forget," I replied. "Dear Charlotte, I know that I can always confide in you. I suppose my mind was so preoccupied that I had quite forgotten myself."

"And this secret that you are keeping? I suppose you shall tell me when you are ready."

"Yes," I agreed, "yes, indeed I shall."

"Very well," she answered, attempting to hide her doubts. She nodded to me and then we watched the Lucas sisters walk down the road before we returned to Longbourn.

"So, you have a secret?" Jane asked me.

"Yes, I do."

"Well, if you wish to keep it, then you may. I shall not press you."

"Thank you, Jane, for I needed only that."

☙❦❧

Into the house we went, and as we did so, I felt my heart and soul not only torn in two still, but so was my mind. Mr. Darcy had been right all along. I had too much foreknowledge, and too much of that was dangerous to one's mental peace. I knew just enough to unsettle me, so that even though I had returned, I had to accept that there was no full way that I would ever go back entirely. A part of me now belonged to the future, and always longed to return.

And for the matter of Charlotte, my knowledge of what she would do would always put me on my guard.

I would doubt her.

I would wonder what she was secretly thinking.

I would also believe that I did not fully know my friend as I had thought that I did.

Charlotte felt it just as I had felt it. There was now a rift between us, and she sensed it, because I did little to conceal it.

In such a circumstance, I felt both unfortunate for her and for myself. I wished that we could return to what we were, with her as my dear friend who I told everything to, as well as she being willing to be confided in, but I suppose time had to help me in that circumstance, because I needed something else to heal it.

Or was that why Time had specifically brought me back to my time after it had taken me to that future? As I could only reason with the possibility that I had woken up in that era because I had to help Mr. Darcy from making the biggest mistake of his life, maybe the only reason for why I was returned to my own world was because I had to make sure that we did not lose Longbourn. Thus, I could not help but wonder if I was mainly brought back to save my family *from* my own friend.

# Chapter Three

## THE FIRST DANCE

As was the way it is with proper manners and habit, we Bennets soon waited on the ladies of Netherfield, and very quickly my judgment of both sisters was cemented in stone. Jane quickly became a favorite of Miss Bingley and Mrs. Hurst, but it was clear that Caroline and Louisa thought our mother intolerable and the rest of us sisters not worth speaking to. They were kind toward me enough, but their general air and demeaning ways did not go amiss, and therefore I could not like them.

Yet as Caroline Bingley sat there, and I observed her talking to Jane, I could not help but think to myself:

*Two hundred years from now, I'm going to punch you.*

The thought, I do not deny, still gave me pleasure. Of course, this was a different Miss Bingley, who simply had the same face and figure, but the eye cannot forget so easily. And since her nature was very quickly proving to be supercilious toward everyone except Jane, this prejudice continued to be cemented.

Yet when Mr. Bingley did enter, followed by Mr. Darcy, he made a quick walk toward Jane's place, sat down immediately and began to engage in conversation. Mr. Darcy merely nodded to us all before he took his place standing by the window and looking out of it.

While it was clear that Mr. Bingley truly did admire Jane, and I could not be happier for her, my eyes shifted toward Mr. Darcy. Could he be even remotely similar to his descendent? They had the same face and figure, but did they have the same ability to… change?

At first when I had met my Mr. Darcy, he was conceited a bit, and a little self-centered, but who wasn't every now and again? Yet once I was able to get underneath his skin, I realized that it had only took a little drawing out before he became one of the greatest men that I had ever met. Did this Mr. Darcy simply need a little drawing out? Or he simply needed to know how it felt to be accepted. Well, I wasn't going to figure out just by sitting there, and I wasn't in the mood to ignore every rash and wild instinct that I had before I lost my nerve.

Therefore, I stood up, walked past my mother who was eyeing Mr. Darcy with cold disdain. She clearly was upset that he did not even attempt to speak to us, which could very easily be comprehended. I then accosted him, stood by his side and stared out of the window. This clearly surprised him as he did not expect that.

"Lovely view of the land," I voiced.

"Yes, it is."

"Though I am sure that this prospect does not boast half so well as a view from Pemberly, but still, you cannot deny that Hertfordshire has its share of beauties."

"It does, indeed," was his only reply.

Dear lord! Pulling words from him was like drawing water from stone. And then I realized what did I have to lose? Truly there was nothing at stake for me, for I had no intention of having him fall in love with me, or me falling in love with him. My heart had very much belonged to another and would remain that way. All that I could do, at this point, was get to know him and make sure to always find out what was occurring within him, for any day, he would disappear without a trace, and I had to know how to help him, if I could.

Or if he would let me, of course. Therefore, I breathed in heavily and began to breach propriety in every way. Yet, indeed, it would not be the first time.

"At first I thought it was because you were rude," I began, to which Mr. Darcy ceased his fierce and fixed gaze out of the window and focused on me.

"Pardon?"

"Your coldness," I remarked. "I thought it was because you were rude. Insufferably rude. I believed that you did not care for the feelings of any around you, hence why you were so desirous to give offense at the ball, and perhaps even why you were above being pleased. But now I wonder if I was too hasty in my judgment. Now I wonder if you are a good man underneath, and you simply have the popular fault of just being very shy, very bashful."

I looked at him as his eyes bore sternly into mine.

"You think that I ought not to speak so?" I asked.

"I think you have been thinking on me a great deal," was his only reply.

"Perhaps I have, but I make no apologies for my roaming mind. Am I wrong, then? Are you not just simply shy? If it be not so, if you are just a stone, a statue and this is where you wish to stand, then never mind, sir. And I shall leave you to it."

I began to walk away, but then I heard him shift, so I turned around and he had in fact taken a step toward me.

"I was merely trying to understand you," I continued, "no more and no less. You had nothing to lose."

I curtsied to him and then walked back to the main company.

As I did so, I both saw and felt Caroline Bingley's eyes upon me, and it was a look of pure venom. Then she stood up, left Jane's side while Mrs. Hurst spoke with her, approached Mr. Darcy and began to speak with him, keeping him there at the window.

As they talked, I noticed more that she spoke and Mr. Darcy either gave her quick replies or just simply did not respond. I wanted to laugh at her attempts at flirting, for that is what it was. Seeing her with him, it became clear once more, that even in this time, Caroline Bingley considered Mr. Darcy as the proper object to pursue.

With this being the only parallel to the future and my present, I wondered if that was another reason for why I had been returned to my own time. Was I to come back simply because I had to shield Mr. Darcy once more from making a mistake? No, I answered my own question, for that was one small man's dilemma. Something else was at work, something unknown.

Yet as our visit came to an end, Mr. Darcy and Mr. Bingley escorted us to the carriage along with the sisters and Mr. Hurst. As they did, Mr. Bingley spoke with Jane the whole time, and I remained with my sisters. Yet as I stood there, I felt Mr. Darcy's eyes upon me while he stood next to Caroline Bingley, and at first, I did not look. Yet I was curious, so I turned to him, and as I suspected, he was looking at me in earnest. As he did so, I noted him in return, and I also noted Miss Bingley watching him as he was watching me. Aye, there was a triangle of stares, Mr. Darcy surprised me as he continued to look on me without shame, and I only returned his stare with the intense one of my own.

At last, we were to enter the carriage, we did so, and then we rode off to Longbourn.

The later part of the week brought a party at Lucas Lodge, and when our family arrived, we found that the Netherfield company was already there. Mr. Bingley immediately sought out Jane. She was happy to see him, and I was left to walk around and converse with others. As I did so, I noticed that Mr. Darcy was always quite near me, but he never fully approached. While I could have helped him on, I thought it best to let him be as he liked, and only speak to me if he so desired. So, when he clearly eavesdropped, I did nothing, nor made any remark toward him. My sister, Mary, was playing the pianoforte, where eventually all asked her to play a jig so that Lydia and those who wished to dance could do so.

"I prefer not to just now," Mary stressed.

"Oh, don't be *you* right now," Lydia whined, "and come on then."

"I'd rather not, just to disoblige you."

Lydia rolled her eyes and then turned to our mother, but Sir William interfered before my mother could add her voice to the matter.

"Oh, please, Miss Mary," he said. "Let us all give into their fancies for just this once, so that the Netherfield Party may hear how accomplished you are in this regard."

This was the perfect way to appeal to Mary, who lived off of such compliments, yet when considering the need for every human to receive respect for their accomplishments, Mary was no more self-indulgent than either of us, and I suppose that I had to remember that. Therefore, glad to purchase praise and gratitude by Scotch and Irish airs, at the request of our younger sisters, who, with some of the Lucases, and two or three officers, joined eagerly in dancing at one end of the room, Mary began to play.

As they did so, I looked to a corner where Mr. Darcy was standing alone, looking on the scene with silent indignation. And yet Sir William Lucas, always willing to be obliging, accosted Mr. Darcy and offered him one more chance to prove himself not to be the most taciturn man to ever walk into Hertfordshire.

"What a charming amusement for young people this is, Mr. Darcy! There is nothing like dancing after all. I consider it as one of the first refinements of polished society."

"Certainly, sir," Mr. Darcy replied. "And it has the advantage also of being in vogue amongst the less polished societies of the world. Every savage can dance, sir."

Sir William did not know how to reply to this, for who would? Therefore, he only smiled, commented on how Mr. Bingley was a fine dancer, he observed, for at that moment, Mr. Bingley and Jane joined the dance.

"I doubt not that you are adept in the science yourself, Mr. Darcy," Sir William added.

"You saw me dance at Meryton, I believe, sir."

"Yes, indeed, and received no inconsiderable pleasure from the sight. Do you often dance at St. James's?"

"Never, sir."

"Do you not think it would be a proper compliment to the place?"

"It is a compliment which I never pay to any place if I can avoid it."

*Mr. Darcy, of course you would say that.*

At that point, I saw Charlotte approaching me, therefore I thought it best to leave my place to pretend as if I was walking to my mother, in hopes of not encountering Charlotte at that time, for fear that she would ask me of the secret that I only pretended to have.

Yet as I did so, I passed nearby Sir William, his eye was caught and then he called out to me.

"My dear Miss Eliza, why are you not dancing?" He took my hand and before I knew it, he was leading me toward Mr. Darcy, whose eyes appeared to flash as I neared him.

"Mr. Darcy, you must allow me to present this young lady to you as a very desirable partner. You cannot refuse to dance; I am sure when so much beauty is before you."

As he presented me to Mr. Darcy, I knew Mr. Darcy's sentiments all too well, therefore I did my best, trying to suppress any feelings of discomfort, to resist the offer kindly.

"Indeed, sir, I have not the least intention of dancing," I stated. "I entreat you not to suppose that I moved this way in order to beg for a partner."

"Then you do not wish to dance at all?" Mr. Darcy asked, to my surprise, and I replied with all alacrity.

"I only dance when the partner is of the same mind as I am. Therefore, I only dance with those whom I wish to dance with, and for those who wish to dance with me."

Mr. Darcy swallowed and then replied with grave sincerity, "If you would give me the pleasure, then I would be very happy if you were to dance with me, Miss Elizabeth."

"Even when it is not a compliment you would bestow on any place if you can help it?" I asked archly.

"I am willing to bestow it now. If you would do me the honor."

"Very good sir," Sir William said. "Capitol! Capitol! You excel so much in the dance, Miss Eliza, that it is cruel to deny me the happiness of seeing you, and though this gentleman dislikes the amusement in general, he can have no objection, I am sure, to oblige us for one half-hour."

"Well," I decided, making a choice, "if Mr. Darcy wishes to dance, then I shall be happy to oblige him."

Taking my hand in his, Mr. Darcy led me to the dance floor. As we walked, heads began to turn, my mother's included. As I walked to the dance floor with Mr. Darcy, she whispered in our Aunt Phillip's ear, and then we entered the set next to Mr. Bingley, who smiled at his friend.

"Well," Mr. Bingley said with a chuckle. "You are no longer as fastidious as you were the other day, I see."

"Oh Charles," Mr. Darcy grumbled, but a smile escaped him briefly. We entered the set with grace, and then began to dance.

"So, your friend is the only one who can make you smile, I see," I noticed.

"Well, he is my closest friend, I suppose," Mr. Darcy replied, much to my surprise.

"I did not expect such a reply from you," I admitted.

"What sort of reply did you expect?"

"A guarded one. Or should I say a proper one, but never an honest one. Do not mistake me, I do not assume that you aren't a sincere man, believe me, I know you to be full of veracity, even if it be harsh. I just did not expect you to be as such so very quickly into the dance, if at all."

"You began this strange sort of exchange of confessions, therefore I thought there was nothing to fear in following suit. Though I do not deny at first, your behavior has quite discomforted me."

I slanted him a glance. "Have I frightened you?"

Mr. Darcy looked at me even more directly. "Why do you ask such questions?"

"Because something tells me that you actually wish for me to ask you these sorts of questions, but you are too proper to admit it."

"And you are not so?"

"No, I am not. Because, for the moment, it would do no good to be so. Do I startle you in the sense that I am willing to ask you such questions?"

"I would by no means sustain any pleasure of yours."

"Mr. Darcy is all politeness," I replied in jest.

"Do you mock me now?"

"Why do you manage to find offense at everything when there is no offense given?" I replied, a little graver, "What happened to you that you are determined to go through the world willing to be displeased?"

"Are you the sort to be in a rage of acceptance of everyone that you meet?" he asked.

"You answered my question with a question, which was not as polite as one would hope. Yet, if someone has given me no reason to despise them, then I am not the sort to look for a reason. No, I prefer to believe in people until they give me no choice but to not find them so very agreeable."

"So, you never find anything worth judging?"

We followed the dance steps, and despite myself, I had to admit he danced quite well.

"Oh, there is always something worth judging, I am sure, and I find it quite often. Yet I choose to despise only those who give me no choice but to find them despicable. Who here in Hertfordshire has given you reason to believe them to be?"

He frowned. "When did I say that they did?"

"You appear to be the sort to judge harshly, by your own admission, if you do not mind me saying so."

"I confessed to as much, therefore I shall never deny such, but too oft it is the custom for those to not observe the true natures of those around them."

I nodded. "And you believe that you discern clearly."

"I do believe that I do possess some powers of discernment, as you boast of it."

I gave him a look of surprise. "Me? Boast?"

"Yes, you do Miss Bennet, but in secret, I believe that you find yourself quite proficient in observing the follies and true intentions of those around you."

"You profess to think that you know me a great deal, Mr. Darcy?"

"I do believe so. For as you have shown, you believe me to be bashful."

"Was I wrong then? Was I wrong to believe your intentions were better than what they can be misconstrued as? Or do you just not enjoy the company and have no desire to?"

His demeanor closed. "I… I do not wish to speak of such things now."

"We have been open so far, and now you close yourself off so very suddenly. Yet what more could I ask for? After all, how was I to expect you to reveal your true nature to a woman who you found tolerable, but not handsome enough to tempt you?"

His head turned to me sharply and I only smiled gently.

"Come now, Mr. Darcy, I was sitting right nearby when you and your happy friend made your remarks. Did you not think that I would not overhear you?"

"Well, I…"

The music came to an end and so did the dance.

Once the dance ceased, we all bowed and curtsied to each other, then we clapped for Mary's playing. As we stood in the set, I looked to Mr. Darcy, whose face was set in stone.

"Now you look afraid of me," I said at last. "Very good. For now, it shows me that you are very much as human as the rest of us."

I then walked away from him, feeling his eyes following me. Whether he would have followed after me, I knew not, for very soon, Kitty came up to me and whispered conspiratorially.

"You danced with Mr. Darcy."

"I cannot tell. All that I can say is that *he danced with me*, but I cannot say so successfully that I danced with him."

"And by that you mean that you danced, but there was something wanting? There was a lack of connection somewhere."

I gasped, surprised. "Yes. I did not know that you would have understood my meaning."

"Oh, for god sakes, Lizzy, always the tone of surprise when I say something intelligent. It really does hurt."

"Yes," I allowed, acknowledging that perhaps I had not fully seen many things as I ought to have at one time. "Yes, I suppose that it does."

"Well," she replied, "this I can tell you. I think he is trying to make amends for what he did, for he clearly did not wish to dance unless it was with you."

"He felt pressured."

"He barely spoke to Mrs. Robinson when she talked to him, so he is accustomed to refuse anything that he does not want. So be prepared for him to possibly improve on closer acquaintance. Oh, and just to warn you, Charlotte knows that something is amiss between you both."

I flinched. "I beg your pardon?"

"Yes, she knows that you are upset with her over something or the other."

"But…but Kitty, you noticed this?"

"Of course, I noticed this, for I have been your sister for my entire life, you know. I do believe that I quite know you by now."

What a surprise it was! To think that I had once valued myself on my powers of discernment, and for all that time to know Kitty and not know Kitty. Often our father remarked on Kitty and Lydia as being two of the silliest women in the country, but being in another world, in another time, where young women of their age were understood to be that way, I just began to realize that Kitty could very well be the average and actually ideal teenager.

She was at a very trying age, where she was figuring herself out, for she was only seventeen. In our time, we were expected to grow up so quickly, but in the 21$^{st}$ century, it was implied that one was still undergoing growth through trial and error. Kitty, like the rest of us, was expected to go from being a child to being a full-fledged mature and composed woman.

Yet when one does that, there is a large gap in there, a missing piece, and that is the link between being a child and turning into a woman. There was no room for discovering oneself in our time, but in the future, there would then be much more time to do so, and it was healthier than it was in the present. And now that I looked on my history with Kitty, she and Lydia had their foolish moments, but they were the moments of teenagers who were at the height of being spirited, and having the youthful energy that one ought to have at that age. And while Lydia did require proper parenting, and much discipline inflicted, Kitty was another matter. In my quickness to judge her merely as being thoughtless and silly, I did not, like many others, note that was just the way of her age, and she had not only some good qualities, but moments of insight and introspection.

"Kitty, thank you," I said. "And I know that you have much wisdom to you."

When I said this, Kitty was surprised and then she smiled. "Oh, no one ever says that about me. "

"Well, you do have wisdom. And you are right, I am hiding something."

"And you don't want to tell me, do you? You just want to tell Jane."

"Even Jane doesn't know."

"Really?" Kitty said, her eyes widening. "Well then, this must be a great secret. But don't tell me, because I'm sure if I knew it, it would only be a matter of time before Lydia tries to pry it out of me."

"You know you can't keep a secret?" I laughed. "Well, you are one of the first women that I know who has ever known that about herself."

Kitty bit her lip and then blushed.

"I am not so very silly, you know. I know father says it a lot, but I am not."

"No, you are just young."

"Precisely. Why must we all be so dead and dull all the time to be sophisticated? I just feel so happy this way, and those who lack any sort of spirits never appear to be happy about anything. I don't want to be unhappy just so that people can say nice things about me."

"I can very well see that."

Kitty, to my surprise, remained near me, talking, and it was as if she was so happy to finally be telling people what she secretly was feeling about things after so very long. I let her do this, because not only did I find such unsuspecting pleasure from it, but I also was able to remain away from the stern and fixed gaze of Mr. Darcy, who spent the rest of the evening looking at me, but not coming up to me, and then also avoiding any tete e tete with Charlotte, who was waiting for a moment to speak to me, and I still had nothing to say.

As the evening was drawing to a close, I saw Caroline Bingley whispering something to Mr. Darcy, and then their eyes turned directly to me, and it was clear. They were talking about me in some way, and about something, so I avoided their looks and continued to leave.

"Whatever it is that is causing this rift between you and Charlotte though, Lizzy," Kitty whispered to me, "you must do your best to end the evening with her being above or below suspicion, you know. Tell her something, be it innocent or substantial. You don't want to push her away."

"When did you get this considerate?"

"And once more," Kitty said with a groan, "tone of surprise. I probably always was this way, but you never asked for my advice until now. Kitty, the Advice Giver, yes, I like that title actually. Yes, I like it very much."

She moved away from me, then went to Lydia, and began to speak with a set of our neighbors before we left. When the time came to leave, I went to retrieve my shawl, and as the servant handed it to me along with my bonnet, I dropped my bonnet on the floor, only to see it roll at the feet of a pair of familiar shoes.

Mr. Darcy then leaned down, picked up my bonnet and took the few steps toward me, handing it over.

"Thank you," I replied softly, as I placed it on my head.

"It is…"

"What?"

He swallowed once more, and it seemed as if he was having a hard time speaking.

"Your bonnet, it is quite lovely."

"Thank you. At Longbourn, we actually like to design our own bonnets. It is… a good way to pass our time."

"Yes, I can imagine it is."

Upon my honor, why did I tell him that? It was such a worthless thing to say, it was awkward, and it appeared as if at Longbourn we never did anything of use. Yet I said it and there was nothing else that could be done.

"Of course, we have many other activities that are industrious and of use," I pointed out, "and…and now I am explaining myself, and I wonder if I even need to."

He gave me a curious look. "What does such a statement pertain to?"

"It pertains to the fact that something tells me that you need no explanation. I want to believe… that you are not judging me at this current moment. I think all that you are doing now is just wishing to talk."

"Yes," he whispered, "yes that is all."

"Lizzy!" Our mother cried. "Come then, it's time to go home. So, come along! Come along then."

I curtsied to Mr. Darcy and then left with my family.

# Chapter Four

## THE HANDSOME FACE

A s we were leaving Lucas Lodge, and I passed Charlotte, now was as good a chance as any, so I gracefully embraced her arm and had her walk with me.

"Charlotte, I do believe that I just danced with Mr. Darcy."

"Yes, you did." Charlotte smiled, eager to speak of it. "And how was it? Was he agreeable or disagreeable?"

"I still cannot tell yet, for it was a mixture of both states. I cannot tell if I made him like me by the end or made him positively despise me."

"Well, he looked at you a great deal after you danced."

"You noticed?"

"He is a hard man to miss, and he did not hide his looks as gracefully as he ought to have."

"Well, it still is unclear. For a person can stare often at someone because they admire them, or stare at them because they loathe them. I have seen both and have been at the mercy of both. But if he hates or admires me after this, I am prepared."

"Lizzy," she whispered, "is this what you were afraid to talk to me about? Were you hiding any feelings you may have had? Because if so, then I would be the last person in the world to call any such feelings foolish."

"Oh, no, that was not it," I said. I searched my mind for the perfect lie, and then I rested on the only thing that I could concoct. "I was beginning to try and write a book."

"You were?" Charlotte asked, eager. "Really?"

"Yes, but I was positively horrid at it, I have abandoned the idea entirely, and now it is over and done. That is why I needed time alone."

"Oh, well, I am sure that it is not so bad as you think, but truly, Lizzy, I am ever so glad that this is all. In truth, for a time, I was worried that you had grown tired of me and therefore was leaving me behind."

When seeing her pitiable looks, I took her hand, feeling very sympathetic.

"Charlotte, you are my dear friend, and I shall never grow tired of our camaraderie."

Content with that, Charlotte bade us farewell and we were off. As our carriage rode away, I looked out of the carriage window and, to my curiosity, I saw Mr. Darcy come to the door of Lucas Lodge and watch us as we left.

⬥

Once we were home, I went to Jane's room, informed her of what Mr. Darcy and I talked of, she remarked on her happiness that we might come to some sort of understanding, and she also was happy to see that Charlotte and I were quite returned to the way that we were.

"You are nothing if not a good friend, Lizzy," Jane pointed out. "It is so much a part of your identity."

"Yes, I suppose that for a moment, I had quite forgotten myself."

"We all do that from time to time. But I do so wonder, Lizzy, what prompted you to reach out towards her and make amends for the breach?"

"Oh, it is strange, but to my surprise, it was Kitty actually."

I then told her all that had transpired between Kitty and me, and it was quite perplexing that she was not surprised at all.

"Kitty is not nearly as foolish as she is considered," she said. "She is young and spirited, that's all. Indeed, I have always known that, deep down, she had many fine qualities, that, due to the circumstances, she is not always allowed to exercise. Think, Lizzy, truly, when does she ever get the chance, in our house, to show any powers of mental strength?

"Psychological advancement is never the order of the day when all that is discussed is who is the next beau that is to come into the neighborhood, will the militia be settled here, who is handsome, when is the next ball, and why men are more handsome in regimentals rather than normal clothes?"

"I see your point. One's mind cannot enhance when it is always in a place where there is no room for advancement."

"Precisely. Kitty is what Kitty has had no choice but to be, as it is with all of us, I feel. But all things considered, she has much to recommend her."

"And I did not see that. How tragic."

"No," Jane said, "how human."

☙❧

As I lay in bed that evening, I reflected on how far I had come. Rather than allow silence to reign in between Mr. Darcy and me, I had opened up very quickly on how he had wounded me. There was a time when I would have refused to speak about it, but now I hadn't the patience for miscommunication.

Also, as for Charlotte, I now knew that despite my foreknowledge, I could not punish her for her actions that she had not committed yet, especially when I did not know the motive or actions leading up to that decision.

To compile with all this, I was beginning to see my family more clearly, because for them, this was all the present. Yet for me, this was once all the past.

My sisters once were separated from me, therefore, absence was able to make the heart grow fonder of things, or respectful of difference. I could see Kitty clearer now, and Lydia still had her wild moments, but I still saw some loveliness to her lively and childish nature. Mary was just starved for attention, therefore, like Kitty, her flaws came from her having a nature that was not allowed to fully develop or always being given the attention that it needed.

In 2016, with all the terms added to such conditions, also the many counselors in supply for young adults, it showed how we women were not often allowed fully developed minds in our time, because we were not allowed to explore it.

Even my mother's trying habits now no longer seemed so very vexing at all. In fact, my mother's ways, manners and moods were so common to many mothers that I had seen in London on any given day when I was traveling around it and riding through the streets in a taxi.

In our times, she was regarded as being ridiculous and vulgar, but in fact, she very well had her moments of just being a normal mother, taxing us, trying us, and clucking over us with good intentions that did not always produce good outcomes.

How many women I had seen shouting and complaining in public when Mr. Darcy and I were getting ice cream in the future? So, was my mother behind the times of how to behave, or was she simply ahead of it? And my father's character also was a very common one as well.

The only tragic aspect to this concept was that the only way for me to have undergone it was for me to have been technically over two hundred years old.

The next day, there was great merriment as Charlotte and Maria Lucas came to fetch Kitty and Lydia, for the militia were known to be coming into Meryton to have their post there, and all in the village and county were astir with the news of it.

Since Jane and I were there as well, they asked us if we were willing to come with them into town so that we would be among the crowd that welcomed them. Our mother, who usually did not ever care to leave her seat, even was willing to walk with us into town to see this sight.

"Normally I don't like walking here and there, I can assure you," she said giddily as she got her shawl on. "And I would much rather sit at home and rest my poor nerves, but this is different."

I put my arm through hers. "Don't worry, Mama, I am sure that you shall like coming with us."

"Of course, Lizzy, of course. Indeed, yes, for you all never wish for me to walk anywhere with you, so this shall be very merry."

"Oh, well," I said, wondering if all this time our mother also was just a little starved for attention, " if you ever want to come with us to places, we shall like it a lot, Mama."

"Oh really?" she asked, quite surprised.

"Yes," Jane said. "Yes, Mama, you need never worry to ask. We merely thought that you did not wish to ever go anywhere with us."

"Well, usually my nerves are as such…oh, well, sometimes I am very good at forgetting about them over time, so never fear, my dears. Never fear."

As we all walked along, Lydia, Maria and Kitty began to wonder if the men in the regiment would be handsome.

"They shall mostly be handsome, I am sure," Lydia declared. "For a man in a fancy red coat can be nothing less than dashing."

"Well, it still does have much to do with his face," Kitty stressed, "but I do agree."

"And a handsome face to a man wearing regimentals!" our mother declared. "Nothing could be more ideal to look on. I liked a redcoat myself, when I was young. I fancied him a great deal."

"Really?" Maria asked. "What was he like, Mrs. Bennet?"

"Oh, he was so very dashing," our mother replied. "There was nothing like him, it seemed. And he was a good dancer as well."

"Which a young man ought to be," I said, "if he possibly can."

"And he could and did!" Our mother laughed. "Yes, I fancied him a lot. And I do still, in my heart."

My sisters, Charlotte, Maria and I gave each other a look and then giggled. When our mother noticed, she blushed.

"Of course, I love your father," she rushed out, to which we could not hold back our laughter. "Oh dear, you must really believe me."

"We do, Mama," Jane said, "of course you love father."

"Yes, I do. I just... well, we never forget our first loves, that's all."

"That soldier was your first love?" Kitty asked. "Really, Mama?"

"Well, we all have our little attachments. And he even wrote me some very pretty verses. That's why, my dear, when that one gentleman who wrote you those verses," she said to Jane, "I was hoping he would make you an offer, but he did not. It really does go to show you that time can sometimes repeat itself."

Jane offered her solace, while I fell into my mind.

*We never forget our first loves...*

True words. Fine words. And it was quite sad that they were true.

Our mother continued to talk about the 'officer' until we reached Meryton and we then were met by a large crowd of people. Indeed, it was quite enjoyable.

"All of Hertfordshire and Meryton appear to be here!" Lydia roared. "And I love it, for nothing could be more glorious than to see and be seen, I feel."

"Why can't life always be this fun?" Maria giggled as we all found a spot in the crowd. Then as the music began to play and drums sounded, there came the stomping of many feet, and the soldiers in the militia, with their muskets and bayonets began to march through our streets. We all cheered for them as they entered, but they mostly just looked ahead, however their eyes twinkled as they walked.

Lydia counted the handsome faces in the set.

Kitty and Maria merely giggled together.

My mother declared that there was one officer who looked just like the man she loved so very long ago.

Jane was enjoying herself, but in the silent sort of way. But as for myself, I cared little for the men marching in, for there was a face in the crowd, who stood nearby us, and he smiled. As he did so, he turned to me and I was so much completely taken with his appearance that I dropped the handkerchief that was in my hand and it blew away. As it did so, I rushed to retrieve it, but he leaned forward and got it instead. When he raised himself up, and handed it to me, his smile deepened, and I found him to be a thoroughly handsome man.

"It appears that it got away from you," he said.

"Yes, and you saved it," I replied, taking it from him. "Thank you, sir."

"While it is always improper to introduce oneself, I believe I may do so now for the situation calls for it." He tipped his hat.

"Very well, my name is Miss Elizabeth Bennet, sir."

"Miss Bennet, it is my pleasure to make your acquaintance. My name is Mr. George Wickham."

"Well, Mr. Wickham, I do believe the pleasure is all mine."

"I can assure you that it is not. Yet, I have pushed propriety as far as it ever has the right to go simply in speaking to a lady before being introduced, but I felt that I could not help myself." I found him charming.

"Shall you remain in Hertfordshire for the duration, Mr. Wickham?"

"I shall. Therefore, I believe that we shall see each other once more."

"Oh, yes, I believe that we shall."

Mr. Wickham then leaned forward and smiled at me in a very appealing way. "Oh, I am certain that we very much shall."

I blushed, curtsied, then walked away. As I returned to my place by my family, the company had been too busy admiring the officers to notice that I was speaking with a strange man, except for one.

"Did you just talk to that man without being introduced?" Kitty asked.

"Kitty, it was simply by accident."

"First, he was very handsome, so I cannot blame you, and second, the next time I do something ever so slightly against decorum, you cannot chastise me now, can you?" She gave me a sly look.

I swatted at her playfully. "Oh, be quiet."

"No, I shall not."

"Just admire the officers."

She turned her gaze upon them. "That I shall do, with great enthusiasm."

We all watched the officers until they had finished marching, and then eventually returned to Longbourn, where our mother returned to in good spirits, after not having mentioned her nerves once in the entire afternoon.

# Chapter Five

## THE WALK OF INFAMY

Now that the regiment was to be stationed in Meryton for the entire winter, the women of Hertfordshire suddenly found themselves an excuse to never be bored.

Kitty and Lydia would prove to be the chief among the women who spent their days trying to become as acquainted with the officers as they could. Therefore, often they would walk into town, visiting our Aunt Phillips, where they would discover another bit of insight, such as the officers' names and connections.

Mr. Phillips also invited the officers to his home often, and since Kitty and Lydia frequented the house, they eventually became acquainted with the men themselves. Yet I did not pay much attention to their discoveries and adventures, because my mind often wondered to Mr. Darcy. I always secretly kept abreast of further news about the residents of Netherfield, to make sure that Mr. Darcy was doing quite well. To my knowledge, he was alive, whole, and complete, thus there never was cause for alarm. Still wishing to keep to my promise to the Mr. Darcy that I had grown fond of in the future, I felt it still within my duty not to turn my back on this Mr. Darcy, despite that it could be a little hard.

And yet, his mind and mood were hard for me to make out. From all outside appearances, he appeared to loathe me somewhat. Yet in having time to reflect on it, I saw that there was the likelihood that my first assessment was correct in that he was a little bashful, and this led to him being very insecure. And when a person is insecure, it leads to them lashing out at others, which was a behavioral issue that there had been discussion on in the future. When I had to look after Gemma and her brother, this was something that had to be studied when dealing with children. And the psychology behind the actions of an adult were no less complex than that of a child.

Yet, despite all my musings and wonderings, reality came down into Longbourn, and I was most occupied for a time when in between all the talks of officers, a letter arrived from Netherfield Park for Jane. It was sent from Caroline Bingley and Louisa Hurst, who asked Jane to dine with them one afternoon, since the men of the house would be dining with the officers.

Of course, our mother thought it would be a waste of a trip if Jane did not see Mr. Bingley in going, so she devised a plan that Jane ought to go on horseback to Netherfield Park. For it looked like it would rain that day, therefore she would be forced to stay overnight. This unnerved Jane, upset me, amused father, vexed Mary, put Kitty's mind at work, and awoke Lydia's love for bursting out into laughter about anything.

Not only was I a little angry at our mother being so obsessed for devising such a scheme, but also because I did not trust Caroline Bingley. Yes, she would be a different one than the one that I had known, but my prejudice could not be destroyed so very easily, and I found myself not wishing for Jane to be alone with such a woman that Miss Bingley had the potentiality to be.

Yet Jane obeyed our mother and rather than traveling there in a carriage, she took Ruby, one of our horses, to the park. Sure enough, soon rain had followed, and Jane would have been caught in it. This was confirmed the next day when as we ate our breakfast, I had received a letter stating thus:

*My dearest Lizzy,*

*I find myself very unwell this morning, which, I suppose, is to be imputed to my getting wet through yesterday. My kind friends will not hear of my returning till I am better. They insist also on my seeing Mr. Jones, therefore do not be alarmed if you should hear of his having been to mean, except for a sore throat and headache, there is not much the matter with me. Yours, etc.*

"This is incredible," I said as I lowered the letter and stared down the table at my mother. "Well, was Jane getting sick also in your plan, Mama?"

"Oh nonsense, but this is better in some ways," my mother said.

"Better? And how would that be?"

"Well now she shall have to stay longer, won't she? Which means Mr. Bingley is sure to fall madly in love with her."

"Well, my dear," our father added, "if Jane should die, it would be a comfort to know that it was all in pursuit of Mr. Bingley, and under your orders."

"Oh! I am not afraid of her dying. People do not die of little trifling colds. She will be taken good care of. As long as she stays there, it is all very well. I would go and see her if I could have the carriage."

"Well, whenever you do so," I interrupted, "I shall be glad to see her as well, for I wish to go there and look after Jane."

"But the carriage is not to be had at this time," our mother replied, "and you are no horsewoman, Lizzy."

"First, you're right. I'm no horsewoman and really ought to remedy that, but until then, there is no need for any assistance because I aim to walk there."

"How can you be so silly as to think of such a thing, in all this dirt? You will not be fit to be seen when you get there."

"I shall be very fit to see Jane, which is all I want. The distance is nothing when one has a motive; only three miles. I shall be back by dinner. No, I am determined in this matter, and shall not be shaken out of my resolve," I finalized, worried more and more of Jane being at Netherfield for so long alone.

To be around a woman like Caroline Bingley for an afternoon was not detrimental.

Yet to be around her for at least half a week felt frightful to me.

"I admire the activity of your benevolence," Mary stated, "but every impulse of feeling should be guided by reason. And in my opinion, exertion should always be in proportion to what is required."

Kitty groaned. "Mary, really, now is not the time. Lizzy, Lydia and I will walk you as far as Meryton."

"Brilliant," I said. "I would like some company."

The three of us set off together, and once we reached Meryton we parted ways; I toward Netherfield Park, and Kitty and Lydia toward the lodgings of the officers' wives.

"Promise me that you shall not do that despicable act," I said to them both.

"What despicable act?" Kitty asked.

"That despicably devious act of dropping something on the ground so that an officer shall pick it up and therefore you shall be introduced to him."

"Oh, I like that idea!" Lydia cried.

"Oh dear." I wished then that I had not said anything.

"And now you wish that you had never said anything," Kitty realized.

"Perhaps."

"Oh Lizzy…"

They waved goodbye to me and then we separated at last as I was therefore once more on the road.

Walking alone, crossing field after field at a quick pace, jumping over stiles and springing over puddles with impatient activity, I found myself at last within view of the house, with weary ankles, dirty stockings, and a face warm from activity.

My assumption was that I was going to first and foremost accost the house, be shown into the parlor and be met by many blank expressions of surprise at me being there. But it was not so. In fact, the very first face that I had seen was as I passed through the lands onto the Netherfield grounds, there was a solitary walker and I came face to face with…

"Miss Bennet!"

"Miss Bingley!"

There before me was the alarmed Caroline Bingley, completely unhappy to see me.

"Good Lord, Miss Bennet!" Caroline exclaimed. "Whatever do you do here?"

"Good day, Miss Bingley." I bowed to her, refusing to forget my manners. "I am come to inquire after my sister. For this day I have received a letter stating her ill state, and I wish to attend to her."

"You came here?"

"To look after my sister, yes."

She gave me an odd look. "On foot?"

"Yes, indeed, as it can be observed."

"You walked here, from Longbourn?"

"Yes, from Longbourn," I informed her.

"And just how far is that?"

"About three miles."

"You walked three miles."

"Yes."

"Three whole miles," she repeated.

"Walking is always beneficial exercise."

"When not done to excess."

"I have never found walking something to be done too much of."

She then only stared at me and did nothing else at all.

"Forgive me," I said, trying to hide my annoyance, "but would you be so kind as to take me to her?"

"Yes, well," she replied, dubious of me, "yes, I suppose I can."

She turned around and I began to follow her into the house.

"So, walking three miles because your sister has a cold. My dear, that is quite a unique feat, is it not?"

"I suppose it can be viewed as such. How does my sister do?"

She began to look sad. "Oh, indeed, it is a most unfortunate thing. Your poor and sweet sister. We feel quite alarmed by it, for she is quite ill, and we do hope that she recovers. It has been a very short acquaintance, but we do dote on her and find her to be a lovely and gentle girl. Very sweet and *always following the ways of proper decorum*. Nothing *there* to reprimand, I declare."

I knew and sensed the hidden meaning behind her words, and I cared not for it, but only looked on her most pleasantly.

"Yes, she is always so very good," I confirmed, "hence my worry. When having a sister of such sweet gentleness, she deserves all the sisterly affection that one ought to give."

Caroline smiled diplomatically and said no more as we walked onward. As we did so, I had no scruples in looking at her, determining her character, and letting all my inner frustrations release. I still did not trust her, and I knew, even then, that I was right not to.

When I was presented to the rest of the company in the breakfast-parlor, my appearance was met with a great deal of surprise.

I was quite convinced that Miss Bingley and Mrs. Hurst held me in contempt for it. Mr. Hurst did not say anything to me at all, but Mr. Bingley was ever so nice and appeared to be happy with my appearance. The only person who was absent was Mr. Darcy.

"Miss Bennet has slept quite ill," Mrs. Hurst reported to me, "and while she is awake, she is feverish, and not well enough to leave her room. If you like, we can have one of the servants take you up to her room."

"That would be very good of you," I acknowledged as Louisa called for a woman named Shelby and Shelby escorted me up the stairs. As we walked, only then did I notice that the hem of my petticoat was very much covered in dirt and mud. I was certain that the sisters were quite ripping my reputation to shreds down below, and there was nothing for it.

Yet as Shelby was leading me up the stairs, any mystery of where Mr. Darcy could be was answered as he appeared at the top of the steps, with a book in his hand. When we beheld each other, we both stopped in our tracks, with him at the top of the steps and me in the midst of it.

"Miss Bennet!"

"Good day, Mr. Darcy." I smiled, curtsying. "Yes, I am here. And now excuse me."

I continued to follow Shelby up the steps, Mr. Darcy remembered himself enough to move for us, we passed him and then we walked down the hallway. Despite myself, I could not resist giving him a backwards glance. As I did so, I was content in seeing that he was looking at me in wonder or disgust. With his sort of expressions, it was quite hard to tell.

When I entered to find Jane most unwell, her spirit lifted as she saw me.

"You came for me." She smiled, hoarse.

I hurried to her side. "Of course, I did, dear Jane."

I was there to tend to her, though she was too ill to speak much, but I was happy in that at least I could keep her company. The Bingley sisters came to visit her every now and again, their concern did appear to be somewhat genuine and they did express love for Jane. This did potentially raise my esteem for them in my eyes, but I was also prepared for them to do something eventually afterwards to lower my expectations of them.

The apothecary came, determined that she had a violent cold and that she ought to remain in bed at the house. Jane requested that I stay with her, and to my surprise, Miss Bingley agreed to this, though I would not be surprised if it was at the pressing of Mr. Bingley. Therefore, the carriage was sent to bring my clothes.

Eventually Mr. Bingley himself visited Jane's sick room, and to my surprise, he was joined by Mr. Darcy. This sort of behavior breached propriety, but we cared not at all, it seemed. As Mr. Bingley sat near Jane and talked, I thought it would be wiser to move away from them, give them one moment of intimacy and so I stood up, went to a window and looked out. As I did so, I could not help but steal a glance at Mr. Darcy once more. When quickly looking upon him, I faltered when I saw that his gaze was also upon me, so I turned my eyes away immediately and once more looked out of the window. As I did so, I was surprised when I heard him stand up, accost me and also look out of the window.

"You find me doing one of your favorite activities," I noted, "looking out of the window in deep thought."

"In truth, I do it when I have no idea what else to do or say," he replied, and I turned to him, a sly smile upon my lips.

"Did you just give me an honest answer?" I asked.

"I always give you an honest answer to things."

"Yes, you do, but that one was one that I did not have to pull out of you. I do believe we are learning how to survive each other."

He cocked his head at me. "Did you require learning how to survive me, Miss Elizabeth?"

"Yes, I confess that I did," I admitted, and this time it was his turn to be surprised.

"Why so?"

"Because I have a love for illustrating characters when I meet them, and I am attempting to make yours out. But I cannot get on at all; therefore, I do not know what to make of you."

"I declare that I am very simple. You have discovered a lot sooner than most, that my chief weakness is bashfulness."

"And mine is cheekiness," I noted, smiling. "And I suppose that it shall always be so."

"Is that the flaw you put to your great walk here? Your walk of infamy?"

"Is that what you are all saying about it down below? You are calling my walk infamous?"

"Well, I said no such thing."

"Really?" I asked dubiously. "Why do I doubt that?"

"You ought not to. I was surprised by your journey, I do not deny this, but it was a marked change to what I am used to. And I shall admit to this, Miss Elizabeth."

"Admit to what?"

"You amaze me in that you do not fear much."

"It has more to do with experience rather than natural expertise. I have had enough experiences, Mr. Darcy, to last me for a lifetime. I suppose, there is nothing left for me to be afraid of."

"But you admitted to being unnerved by me?"

"I am, for you are quite an unknown. Not so much a mystery, but a sort of enigma. I feel as if I shall know you, but also never know you, that we shall exchange pleasantries, and still not fully ever learn to find each other pleasant. We shall be polite, but never more than forced politeness. What I mean, Mr. Darcy, is that we shall tolerate each other, but that is it."

"What are you saying?" He leaned more toward me. "Do you really believe that I hold you in contempt?"

"What other logical judgment can I make from a man who has claimed to find me not worthy enough to dance with?"

"I danced with you at Lucas Lodge."

"You were forced to."

"No one ever forces me to do anything," he stated flatly, to which I couldn't help but laugh.

"Is that so?" I asked.

"Yes, it very much is. I despise being forced to do as I do not like."

"And you didn't want to dance with me."

"At first, but then I did wish to dance with you afterwards, so I did."

"And what brought about this changing of your mind?"

"In truth?"

"Yes."

He shrugged. "I have no idea."

I scoffed and had to immediately stifle the sound of it by coughing. When I felt that I had quite covered up my slip from Jane and Mr. Bingley, I turned once more to Mr. Darcy.

"Well," he remarked, "that was nicely handled."

"Thank you," I replied, "but really? That is your answer? You simply have no idea what brought about this change?"

"Well, a part of me doesn't."

"Oh, for god sakes man, do not be elliptical, or coy, for there is no point in being either, and I have seen the errors of not communicating things properly. Indeed, our society is quite backwards in that way, for we praise logic and then embrace the most illogical concept in the world: not ever saying what one really ought to."

He nodded. "Yes, we are a society that has no real idea how to convey our emotions. Yet what more, or less, is there to expect? For indeed, emotions are terrifying to us."

"Because we are so enamored with sense that we reject sensibility on principle. We truly don't understand the delicate balance that is yin and yang."

"Yin and yang?" he asked, confused. "I beg your pardon?"

"Oh, sorry." I bit my lip, realizing that I had used futuristic culture phrasing. "It is a Chinese term that is quite ancient, and it means complements. The complements of things. Now tell me, what brought about this change? And please, do your best not to insult me in the process. Yet if you do, then I shall do my best not to be offended, for I see that sometimes you cannot help yourself."

Mr. Darcy drummed his hands against his thighs.

"Thank you. Miss Elizabeth, the truth is that often, I do mean well."

"We all mean well, Mr. Darcy. The point is, do we attempt to do well. So?"

"I suppose that I quite liked how pretty your eyes were when they were aglow."

"That is it?"

"Yes, a bit. Well, quite a big bit."

I blushed. "Thank you, Mr. Darcy."

"You are very welcome. Of course, it all depends on many things. It is not enough to have a pair of fine eyes, but the way they ignite is all the more. When you smile happily and laugh, your eyes are all alight; I can tell that you are happy, Miss Elizabeth. And what is more, I can tell that the happiness is real. Also, I had gained a larger acquaintance with you. I didn't know you when I rejected you at first. Yet at Lucas Lodge, I did know you better, and therefore I had time to feel more at ease."

"To not make a decision guided by your shyness," I noted.

"Yes, I did. I had more time to be open and to reflect."

"Well, now that I have walked three miles, not fit to be seen, as I am sure that others have noted in the house, I am afraid that this adventure of mine has affected your admiration for my fine eyes."

"Not at all. They were brightened by the exercise."

I looked at him and had to chuckle.

"Well," I said at last, "you are a different sort of gentleman, if you will allow me to say so."

"And you are a different sort of lady," he retorted.

"Then let us try and be friends, Mr. Darcy. I am harmless, and you need have no fear of me. Especially since our companies are to be so intertwined, that we ought to come to an understanding in that way. Let us at least try and get along with each other."

"Miss Elizabeth," he began, looking deeply at me, and then he blinked and looked away. "Yes, yes, I believe that I would like that."

Mr. Bingley then stood up, it was time to leave, and Mr. Darcy followed him out.

# Chapter Six

## A GOOD INSULT

When both men left, I turned to Jane, who smiled weakly.

"What is that look for?" Jane asked me.

"I think, even when you are as sick as you are," I offered, "that Mr. Bingley is well on his way to falling in love with you."

"And with you? I believe that I can say in reply that Mr. Darcy is full on his way to being happy to see you often."

"We merely came to an understanding."

"And a small understanding can go a long way. I may have been talking to Mr. Bingley, but I did my best to be observant, and I noticed how Mr. Darcy approached you and you both spoke a good deal. He was smiling at you often. As you were with him. First, he danced at Lucas Lodge and then this. Whatever will you both think of next? A walk along the meadows of Netherfield arm in arm?"

"You joke, Jane! And you tease."

"I cannot help it, for I do suppose that I am happy for you, Lizzy, and I am proud of you."

"Proud? Why so?"

"Because, despite how abominably he has treated you, you have quickly forgiven him. That is quite incredible to do. To forgive a man who slighted you in such a way."

"Yes, I daresay that I have even surprised myself."

"Well, I always knew that you had such goodness in you, Lizzy. And I am glad of it, and something tells me that so does Mr. Darcy."

"Well, it is best that we do get along, for the sake of you and his friend if for no other reason."

"Lizzy," Jane said, taking my hand softly as I sat down, "don't think of me right now. You have made me so happy already in your coming. You therefore have permission to think of yourself for a mere little."

"All I can think about is if I can survive the running of this household. You know my feelings for Miss Bingley and Mrs. Hurst."

"Well, have you therefore seen how lovely they are treating me?"

"I have, and while this has endeared me toward them a little more, I daresay that I venture to think of them both as I had already thought of them before."

"Well, I suppose I shall have to content myself with that. But truly, Lizzy, I do hope that you become good friends with them eventually."

"Perhaps it is possible. After all, the earth was created in six days, was it not?"

"Aye, it was."

As I went down the stairs with a pitcher, content to find a maid to refill it, my silent footsteps proved to be both the making and undoing of me, because as I walked along, I overheard the conversation of Miss Bingley as she was speaking with Mr. Darcy, Mr. Bingley and the Hursts.

"She has nothing, in short, to recommend her," Mrs. Hurst commented, "but being an excellent walker. I shall never forget her appearance this morning. She really looked almost wild."

"She did, indeed, Louisa," Miss Bingley pressed. "I could hardly keep my countenance. Very nonsensical to come at all! Why must *she* be scampering about the country, because her sister had a cold? Her hair, so untidy, so blowsy!"

"Yes, and her petticoat, I hope you saw her petticoat, six inches deep in mud, I am absolutely certain, and the gown which had been let down to hide it not doing its office."

"Your picture may be very exact, Louisa," Mr. Bingley countered, "but this was all lost upon me. I thought Miss Elizabeth Bennet looked remarkably well when she came into the room this morning. Her dirty petticoat quite escaped my notice."

"*You* observed it, Mr. Darcy, I am sure," Miss Bingley said, "and I am inclined to think that you would not wish to see *your* sister make such an exhibition."

"Certainly not."

"To walk three miles, or four miles, or five miles, or whatever it is, above her ankles in dirt, and alone, quite alone! What could she mean by it? It seems to me to show an abominable sort of conceited independence, a most country-town indifference to decorum."

"It shows affection for her sister that is very pleasing," Mr. Bingley argued, and it made my heart swell that he was willing to defend me in such a way.

"I am afraid, Mr. Darcy," observed Miss Bingley in a half whisper, "that this adventure has rather affected your admiration of her fine eyes."

"Not at all," he replied. "They were brightened by the exercise."

A short pause followed this speech, and I could not help but suppress a laugh. Miss Bingley, along with her snotty sister, was content in being my undoing in whatever era. And for Mr. Darcy to be my champion once more, it was quite warm to feel.

"I have an excessive regard for Miss Jane Bennet," Mrs. Hurst continued after a slight pause in their discussion. "She is really a very sweet girl, and I wish with all my heart she were well settled. But with such a father and mother, and such low connections, I am afraid there is no chance of it."

When hearing that, I saw that I was right all along! Yes, they liked Jane, but if they had any strong regard, then they would not have said such a thing. And to ridicule my family's connections and insult my parents. Yes, they were not perfect, but my parents were *my parents*. Therefore, for anyone to say such things to offend them made me quite irate.

"I think I have heard you say that their uncle is an attorney in Meryton," Mr. Bingley noted.

"Yes, and they have another, who lives somewhere near Cheapside."

"That is capitol," Miss Bingley mocked, and they both laughed heartily.

"If they had uncles enough to fill *all* Cheapside," cried Bingley, "it would not make them one jot less agreeable."

"But it must very materially lessen their chance of marrying men of any consideration in the world," Mr. Darcy replied, and that made me feel cold once more. For Miss Bingley and Mrs. Hurst to be against me was expected. Yet for Mr. Darcy to add such a remark, then he felt, inside, that Jane was not good enough for Mr. Bingley, and therefore I felt immediately defensive.

What was worse was that Mr. Bingley did not reply to this statement, and it showed that Mr. Darcy's argument won the day. Mrs. Hurst and Caroline agreed to this, and therefore gave cold remarks and warm insults to my sister's connections. I was so bitter in hearing this I thought it best to walk away and get the water, not hearing anymore.

When I returned to Jane's room, I put on a brave face and decided that it would be best not to tell Jane what I overheard, for I didn't want to worry her for anything. Therefore, I merely tended to her.

Yet now my troubles had been doubled. What little bit of progress I thought I had made with Mr. Darcy was not as solid as I had hoped. And also, instead of having one demon to worry about, I now had two. Between the cruel characters of both Bingley sisters, I saw myself to be right, and therefore, despite using such futuristically vulgar references, sometimes it could not be helped. And now, I had two bumfaces on my hands.

⚜

At first, I had planned to dine with the Netherfield party, but now, I found that I didn't have the stomach for it. So, I begged them to let me eat with Jane in her bedroom. Therefore, I was able to find the solace of being safe and away from the scrutinizing gaze of the Bingley sisters and even Mr. Darcy.

The next day came, and even before my mother and sisters would come to check on Jane, we were surprised to be visited by the Lucases who came to pay a visit to the Bingleys. They had also heard that Jane was ill.

Yet when they entered, and Charlotte saw me, she was quite surprised as she came up to me and took my hand. Jane, who was feeling slightly better than the day before, also came down to the sitting room and sat with the company for a time. Mr. Bingley was most attentive to her, never leaving her side in the whole time that she was present. As Lady Lucas inquired after her health, Charlotte sat down beside me and watched Mr. Bingley as he spoke with Jane about her favorite books to read.

"It is generally evident whenever they meet," Charlotte whispered to me, "that he *does* admire her and it is equally evident that Jane is yielding to the preference which she had begun to entertain for him from the first."

"And I do believe that she is in a way to be very much in love," I noted.

"Then this serenity of her countenance shall never do and can never do."

I looked at her, surprised. "What do you mean, Charlotte?"

"What I mean is that she is so sedate in her reactions to him, Lizzy. Almost too sedate."

I looked on Jane and saw as she smiled at Mr. Bingley, but admittedly the smile was complacent. Since Jane united, with great strength of feeling, composure of temper and a uniform cheerfulness of manner which would guard her from the suspicions of the impertinent, no one would or could accuse her of feeling a preference for him. This put her above suspicion and yet, was that correct?

"It may perhaps be pleasant," Charlotte added, "to be able to impose on the public in such a case, but it is sometimes a disadvantage to be so very guarded. If a woman conceals her affection with the same skill from the object of it, she may lose the opportunity of fixing him, and it will then be but poor consolation to believe the world equally in the dark. A slight preference is natural enough, but there are very few of us who have heart enough to be really in love without encouragement. In nine cases out of ten, a woman had better show *more* affection than she feels. Mr. Bingley likes your sister undoubtedly, but he may never do more than like her, if she does not help him on."

As I looked on Jane once more, I began to consider all the women I had met in London in the future, and how it was not only welcome for a woman to show her preference, but it was also expected and desired.

There were many women who actually asked out the men who they were dating, or who proposed, or showed the first signs of attachment. It seemed to be an expected thing, a welcome thing. It did not repulse the man, nor unnerve him. While it could be successfully argued that the gap of 200 years had quite changed the minds of men, women and society as a whole, but the human spirit is usually a very constant and similar thing, even over time.

Perhaps in our times men desired to see a woman's preference for them, but it was simply a standard, a policy that we ought to do the reverse. Men were expected to do all the wooing, but did they always wish to? Did they never desire us to take initiative in any way? Perhaps, we ought to start somewhere with them.

"At first, I believed that she did help him on, as much as her nature will allow."

"Remember, Eliza, that he does not know Jane's disposition as you do."

"Precisely," I agreed. "And I do believe that you may be right on this matter. I shall talk to her."

"Good, for she really ought to snatch him up, for he, like most men, is not a constant. He could very easily leave this place, never return, unless he has something to draw him here. Jane deserves this, but if she does not fight for it, if she does not show it, then how can she gain?"

"Yes, if she does not fight."

I looked at Charlotte, and in seeing how she was willing to assist Jane in such a way, hoping Jane would secure him, it was clear that she did care about my family's future. Whatever led to her marrying Mr. Collins in the end, it would not have been through malice or coldness. There was no way of knowing what it was, but for now, seeing her willingness to serve the best interests of my family, I could forgive her for anything.

"Thank you, Charlotte," I acknowledged. "Your words are that of a good friend."

"Of course, but naturally I would not want Jane to lose such a great opportunity, as I would not wish for you to make such a mistake either." She smiled and patted my leg. "Advise her as soon as may be."

I looked at Caroline Bingley, Mrs. Hurst, and Mr. Darcy, who had just been observing me with Charlotte, and then looked away immediately. Well, our family's connections may be lower than theirs, but still, we Bennets would not give up without a fight!

Once the Lucases left, Jane returned to her bedroom, and therefore I went alongside her, tending to her. Yet once we were alone, I immediately began to administer Charlotte's advice to Jane, who sat there in wonder. When I finished, she looked at me, puzzled.

"Am I really so reserved, Lizzy? That my feelings for him are not so visible?"

"Oh," I faltered, "you did not know that your feelings were not visible? I thought the serenity of your countenance, the modesty of your ways, was known to you."

"I do not deny that I do conceal things to a certain degree, but do I not often smile when I see him?"

"Yes, you do, but how often do you, well, flirt in return?"

Jane covered her mouth. "Flirt? But Lizzy…"

"I do not mean for you to be vulgar in any manner at all. Yet smiling is not enough. One can smile at anyone, whether we are in love or not.

When do you ever look at him in a way that shows your preference for him? When do you tell him anything to implore him to believe that you will always look forward to seeing him again?

"I am not asking you to change your personality, nor to be vulgar, nor to shower him with superfluous flattery that shall appear as forced, but to merely… act. To do, to not be afraid of the feelings you have. And to not be afraid to take what is within, and when it is only the two of you around, to bring it outwards. To show him what you feel."

Jane's eyes were big. "But Lizzy, we are not taught such a thing."

"Really, because when last I looked, our mother was very outspoken. And look, she caught our father."

Jane blinked when she thought on this.

"But Lizzy, I love our parents so terribly, but is their marriage the sort that I ought to aspire to? Do not disbelieve that I love them both…"

"But they are not the best example of domestic felicity. Well, Jane, though I am not married, the fact is that there is no real such thing as perfect domestic felicity.

"Believe me when I tell you that there shall always be vexation and grief between marriage partners. We cannot all be perfect. Therefore, while our parents are not the very model for marriage, perhaps they are not so erroneous an example as we believe. Perhaps they are just simply what people are like when they get married. Time teaches you to both nag and adore the other. Maybe the flaw is not that we cannot achieve perfection, but rather that we look for it.

"Sometimes images of perfection get in the way of seeing what is really there. And while your disinterested ways are always so angelic, perhaps it does not always show Mr. Bingley that you care. How is he to know what is in your heart, Jane? Unless you voice it. He does not know your character as we do. So, show him what is inside of you."

"But, Lizzy, I do not know how to do that."

"I know, it's hard, but truly Jane, I'm not asking you to change. I am merely asking you to reveal what you are to him."

"But you are forgetting something."

"And what is that?"

"What happens if I do show him how I feel, and he does not feel for me in the same way? What if it turns out that he was merely enjoying my company, with no desire for a more permanent attachment? What if he is afraid of my feelings? Or will be upset if I show them? What if my very vigorous emotions chase him away?"

"Well, he ought to feel for you in that way, if he has any sense. And as for the rest, such as if he doesn't, well, in truth, that's a risk that you must take. That's a risk we all take when we choose to fall in love. We risk our hearts, and sometimes it does not work out. It is not that we won them; sometimes that is not what it's about. No, it's about if you ever had the courage to try to begin with, I suppose."

I leaned toward her. "Jane, are you trying? Do you ever really make a start to Mr. Bingley? Do you ever start the conversation and speak of things that you wish to talk to him about? Do you... just try?"

"I suppose...that I do not."

"Well, try. When he enters the room, do you want to talk to only him?"

"Yes."

"And do you want him to sit down next to you?"

"Yes."

"Do you wish for him to visit you often while you are sick?"

"I do not like for him to see me so ugly, but I do like seeing him."

"That is a brilliant thing to say! To admit that you want to see him, but that you are afraid of him seeing you look hideous! Tell him that when you see him again."

"Lizzy, I cannot!"

"Why not?"

"Because it is not proper."

"Why not? What is offensive about it?"

Jane thought about it and then was silent.

"Right, nothing. It is simply you telling the truth. It's simply you letting him know what you really are. When you smile at him, indicate for him to sit next to you, for you wish for it. It's the truth. It's a good truth. Tell him about things you did when you were a child and you were quite naughty about. Or about how you don't sing because you hated the sound of your voice."

"Lizzy, I was so horrible at it!"

"I think he will forgive you, because you are sharing a secret with him that you never share with anyone else."

Jane thought on it some more. "But what if he runs from me?"

"If he runs, then I'm sorry to tell you this, Jane. But if he does, then he just was not the right man for you."

Once more, the Bingley sisters came to her sickroom and offered their condolences for her state, then were gone after ten minutes of lamenting her suffering, probably to go off and play backgammon or something else.

To my surprise, once more, Mr. Bingley came to visit Jane, and even more to my surprise, he was accompanied by Mr. Darcy. When they entered, Jane smiled broadly.

"Mr. Bingley, you have come back to see me again."

"Why, of course." He appeared content in her cheery mood. "Are you at least doing better?"

"I am slightly better, I declare," she displayed, "helped by the wonderful administrations of draught by the apothecary, and the brilliant company of my sister here. But the comforts that I have experienced at Netherfield Park here are unparalleled."

"Really?" Mr. Bingley seemed pleased. "You enjoy being here?"

"I enjoy it very much, indeed. I only wish that you did not have to see me like this, for I must be positively a fright."

"You are not so," he pressed. "I assure you, Miss Bennet, you could never be anything else but positively radiant."

He cut himself off when he realized that his compliment was perhaps exorbitant.

Jane blushed. "Well, if you think my appearance acceptable, then I am not entirely cast down, and shall not lament anything."

"You ought not to at all. Oh, and Mr. Darcy and I come with news. We received a letter from your mother, and she reports that she shall be coming today to check on your health."

"Oh, that is very good. I can assure her that I am very happy here."

"As happy as I am with you being here, I suppose."

Jane smiled at him. "Thank you. When you make such remarks, I feel less like an imposition."

Mr. Bingley looked amazed, quite forgot that Mr. Darcy was in the room, as well as I, and he pulled up a chair and sat down near Jane, wishing to speak with her only.

In seeing that they were both occupied, I accosted Mr. Darcy.

"Well," I whispered, "I think it best that we continue our post of looking out of the window."

"Right."

And together, Mr. Darcy and I suddenly became fascinated with the prospect out of the window.

"Your sister seems better this day," he observed.

"She is better, I gather," I commented, "and she is happy to be here."

"Is she? Well, I can very well understand that, for this is a comfortable home."

"Perhaps it is not the house that renders it comfortable for her, but instead it is the company. Did you not think of that, Mr. Darcy? That perhaps my sister enjoys your friend's company because he is agreeable."

Mr. Darcy looked at me curiously. "You seem angry with me."

"Perhaps it's because I am."

"What have I done to offend you now? For I appear to do it quite often."

"And I wish that you wouldn't. Really, Mr. Darcy, your change in mindset can be quite alarming sometimes. One moment you denounce my charms and won't dance, and then you will dance and are kind, and then the next moment, I walked down the steps to get my sister some more water, and what do I overhear? You stressing my family's shortcomings to your friend, as if you are desiring to dissuade him from bestowing any affection for my sister."

When I said this, Mr. Darcy flinched, and I decided to pursue the matter.

"And really, Mr. Darcy, what is with you all not bothering to consider speaking your minds behind closed doors? Whenever you offend my family, you always do it where I can overhear you, and with no regard to privacy."

"Ah, so you overheard…"

"Everything. Yes, I overheard everything."

"And now you are irate."

"Would you not be in my case?"

"Miss Elizabeth, what you have to understand is that it was spoken merely from objectivity. The facts are the facts."

I turned to Mr. Darcy and scoffed.

"The facts are the facts?" I echoed quietly. "That is your reason behind such hurtful remarks."

I crossed my arms over my chest. "I shall not wish to confront Mr. Bingley's sisters on the matter, because I find their opinion not worth my concern, and I am their guest. So, I have no choice but to accept it. Yet with you, it is a different matter all the same."

"And how so?" he asked simply. "How am I different?"

"I do not know," I replied, unwilling to answer the question, for it was quite a complicated one. "I just know that you…that you are better than this."

Mr. Darcy looked out the window at this.

"I have unnerved you, I see."

"No," he replied. "I merely am trying to comprehend what it is that you want from me."

"I want you to have some feeling."

"You think I lack the method of emotion?"

"I know that you don't, for who does? I just wish that you had some compassion for those around you, sir. You say the facts are the facts, but look over there, at that bed."

Mr. Darcy turned and looked at Jane and Mr. Bingley.

"Those are not facts sitting there in discussion," I commented. "No, those are people. And sometimes people cannot be held down by such tedious things as facts. We are more complicated than that. Jane and I cannot choose our family. No one can. We were born into the world we are in, and we must make do. Also, our family may not be perfect, you are correct, but they are our family. And we will never have another.

"So I will defend my family, sir, and accept that they are imperfect, as every family is. And if there is a want of connection in my heritage, then I do not believe it lessens us, nor do I wish to. Even if society says the reverse. Besides, one day this world will change so utterly, and such barriers will make no difference when it comes to love."

When I spoke this, I shut my eyes, for I realized that I had said too much. I literally spoke as if I knew the future, which of course, I ought not to have.

"You sound like a dreamer," Mr. Darcy replied, "to believe that one day, birth and connections shall mean little."

"You may say I'm a dreamer, but I'm not the only one." I chewed my lip when I realized that I was very much quoting the famous song, but I figured that since Mr. Darcy would not comprehend anything for which I was referring, it was safe to proceed. "I hope one day you shall join us, and the world will live as one."

"That was very poetic, Miss Elizabeth."

"Thank you. In fact, that was quite by accident, but thank you. And yet, what is your proscription for their financial difference? That your friend does not take my sister for serious consideration? Despite her being a good match for him in regards to their similarity of temper and good nature."

"When I first met your sister, I confess that there was more to it than her lack of connections and situation."

"You had another objection?"

"I did, and now you must promise not to despise me for admitting this."

"I both do and do not despise you, as long as you keep talking. Only when you refuse to take me into your confidence will I rail against you, Mr. Darcy. What other reason do you have for objecting to her?"

"Well, I cannot tell you right now, for I might have been in error, but if you don't mind, give me time, please. When I am ready, I will voice what I had observed."

"But I must warn you, Mr. Darcy, I shall not take this lying down. By no means shall I. She is my sister, sir. I will do everything I can to help her find her happiness. I shall fight for her cause in this."

"Miss Elizabeth, my objections do not come from a taciturn nature, therefore, you must not misunderstand me."

"What am I misunderstanding?"

"The stance of a friend, who is doing everything in his power to protect his closest friend."

When he confessed this, I turned to see Mr. Bingley as he laughed at something Jane had said.

"He is one of my very dear friends, Miss Elizabeth," Darcy admitted, "and I do not have many men in my life that have proven to not only accept my nature, always, but have remained true and loyal. Mr. Bingley is rare, and what sort of comrade would I be if I did not now, or ever, do my best to protect him from being imposed upon or being victim to a mercenary act? Women try to charm him because of his money. I have seen it often. And we men, as with any woman, should not be chosen because of our wealth."

"And how is such a fate worse than a woman not being considered worthy due to her lack of wealth? Are we both not of the same mind, just on different sides?"

Mr. Darcy did not reply to this initially.

"Mr. Darcy, how would you feel if someone disregarded your sister, due to her lacking in wealth and consequence, in the way that the Bingley sisters rebuked my family, and also my sister in the process?"

"When you listened in, did you hear anything that offended you personally?"

"Yes, I did."

"Do not regard it, Miss Elizabeth. Miss Bingley and Mrs. Hurst were just speaking from a place of being critical rather than just being cruel."

"I know their nature. Always have. Always will. Yet do you not understand my viewpoint?"

"I do," he answered at last, "but do you not understand mine?"

"I do. I am happy that you and he are such good friends, for friendship is a strong thing, and yet I have to know now if we are on opposing sides. I am on the side of my sister being allowed to be given a chance. You are on the opposing side where her birth, connections and character ought to be scrutinized and therefore her chances shall be slighter. Are we to be enemies, sir?"

"I do not wish for us to be so."

"Then let us do the only logical thing."

He glanced at me. "And what is that?"

"Leave them alone," I answered, turning to them both as they still conversed. "We ought to let them be. Mr. Darcy, they are adults, and should be able to make their own decisions. Perhaps we ought to remove ourselves, remain in the background, and let them determine their own modes of happiness. Do they not have that right?"

Mr. Darcy turned and observed them both. "I am worried about him making the wrong match."

"And I am worried, that between the minds of Miss Bingley, Mrs. Hurst, and you, that my sister will lose out on making the right match. I do not wish to oppose you, Mr. Darcy. I do not want to be your enemy and I want you as a friend. No more, and no less. Are you afraid of my honesty now?"

"No, I am not."

"Really?" I smiled.

"Yes, I perhaps ought to be, but disguise of any sort is my abhorrence," he acknowledged. "Lies complicate matters. Truth is simple."

"So, you do not mind my impertinence now. Very good."

"Why are you so happy about this?" he asked, his eyes twinkling.

"Because it means that we are getting somewhere."

"Are we?"

"Yes, and I only ask this. Mr. Darcy, please, just let them have their own way, and if you still object to this over time, then I know that you will do as you must, but so shall I. Let us save our angry moments of argument for then."

"You think that we shall eventually oppose each other?"

I smiled archly. "At the rate we are going, I am sure that we shall."

After I said this, Mr. Darcy and I could not help but burst out in laughter. This quite distracted Mr. Bingley and Jane, who turned to us.

"What are you both laughing about?" Mr. Bingley asked, "Is it a good joke?"

"On the contrary, Mr. Bingley," I remarked, "it was merely a good insult."

# Chapter Seven

## GOOD ADVICE

"Well then," Jane said, "we shall let you both keep your insults, for we have only been giving compliments over here."

Mr. Bingley turned to her and smiled warmly.

"I do so wonder if I can complement you enough, Miss Bennet," he admitted.

"And I so wonder if I am worthy of them," she replied, "but I welcome them nonetheless."

"Yes, well, I then know not to stop."

I turned to Mr. Darcy and smirked, then attempted to suppress my smile.

"You are smiling at my expense," Mr. Darcy whispered into my ear.

"Yes, I am," I whispered in reply. "Mr. Darcy, mark my words, I shall beat you in this."

His eyes held twinkling warmth. "Oh, shall you?"

"Yes, I shall, for my sister thinks him wonderful, for all the right reasons. Too many people get married for all the wrong ones, and I shall not let my sister fall into that sad category."

"And I shall not let him fall in that category as well. Too many people find themselves stuck in the worst of places."

Inappropriately, perhaps, I touched his arm. "But promise me that you shall let them try."

"Very well, I promise. Yet if I see anything to indicate that my friend is being taken in, I will not be silent, for my good opinion, once lost, is lost forever."

"That is a failing indeed, and forgive me, but I shall laugh at it."

Again, he gazed at me. "You dearly love to laugh, don't you?"

"It is a very distinct trait that belongs to us Bennets, I suppose, but not to you Darcys."

"Laughing is fine, when there is something worth laughing about. And something to laugh about."

"I do recall overhearing you say something else, I believe," I interjected, my eyes twinkling as I spoke. "For I very much recall you saying that when I appeared here at Netherfield from my three-mile walk, you said that my eyes were brightened by the exercise."

When I spoke this, Mr. Darcy flinched, and he felt quite cornered apparently.

"Oh, that was nothing, it…"

He ground his teeth, I smiled, and he walked away. I do believe that I had won that last interaction.

Eventually, Mr. Darcy and Mr. Bingley had to leave at last, to join Mr. Hurst for the shooting, and therefore we were left alone. When so, Jane looked at me, her smile wide.

"Lizzy, you were correct! And it was such good advice! I think that he liked my being more attentive."

"I suppose you cannot thank me only," I admitted, "but rather, it belongs to our dear friend from Lucas Lodge."

# Chapter Eight

## THE BATTLE OF LIKE-MINDED INDIVIDUALS

The Bingley sisters did visit Jane again of course, showing the tenderness of 'friends in worry,' but I knew that it would evaporate as soon as they left.

Then our mother did come to visit, along with Lydia and Kitty, who both were giddy at the prospect of visiting such a place. When seeing Jane, our mother determined that she ought to remain, for fear of her not being well enough to leave. Of course, this was a bit of an exaggeration. I knew very well that Jane did wish to return to Longbourn, but our mother, in hopes of having her remain there for a bit longer, was willing to determine the illness even worse than it was.

She asked Mr. Bingley to allow Jane to remain longer, and this was to the eternal happiness of herself, the annoyance of the Bingley sisters, the joy of Mr. Bingley, the apathetic attitude of Mr. Hurst, and Mr. Darcy just being Mr. Darcy.

When she finally sat with the Netherfield company for a time, my mother showed her slightly embarrassing side. But to my surprise, she did not do anything to reprimand me at all, whispered her happiness in hearing that I would remain with Jane and even went so far as to compliment me in front of the household.

"When Lizzy first said she would walk to see Jane," she remarked, "I was ever so worried, but my dear Lizzy has always been such a great walker, and her affection for Jane is how I raise my girls to be, so compassionate."

Indeed, I wondered what brought about this change in her attitude, but I could only suppose that with our relationship changing after we saw the officers, she now was seeing me differently. This in fact made me wonder, while my mother could be ridiculous, did she not love me that much because we were not that affectionate toward each other? She, Kitty and Lydia were similar in mindset, and I was not. So, I asked about this to the only sister who I thought, surprisingly, would know.

"Oh, it is very much that," Kitty whispered to me when I spoke to her about this. "You see, you never really do much with her, Liz. Yet when we all went out, and you showed your willingness to have her join us, it made her feel as if you both could very well have something in common. Sometimes you are too much like our father, Lizzy, and you don't let her in. I know she can be trying on the nerves, but she just wants…"

"Attention."

Nodding, Kitty said, "Precisely. And like any other person, attention must be paid to her. Keep being happy about some things that she likes, and believe me, Lizzy, she shall begin to become less snippy and critical of your qualities."

Wondering how Kitty deduced this, I then made a connection.

"Kitty, did you ever feel like attention was not being paid to you?"

"Every single time that our father calls me silly," she replied, her voice shaky. "Lizzy, I do not mean to be silly."

"But it's the only way that you get attention."

"Precisely."

I touched her hand gently to soothe her, thanked her, and then my family was off back to Longbourn while I remained behind with Jane.

Later that evening, when Jane was asleep, I knew that I could not ignore the company of the house forever. So, I dressed nicely, went downstairs to the drawing room, where I found the Hursts and Bingleys playing cards, and the game was *Loo*. I was invited to join them, but I declined it, and just wished to read a book.

"Do you prefer reading to cards?" Mr. Hurst asked. "That is rather singular."

"Miss Eliza Bennet," Miss Bingley declared, "despises cards. She is a great reader and has no pleasure in anything else."

"I deserve neither such praise nor such censure," I retorted. "I am *not* a great reader, and I have pleasure in many things."

"In nursing your sister, I am sure you have pleasure," said Bingley, "and I hope it will be soon increased by seeing her quite well."

"I thank you with all my heart, sir." I was happy in seeing him so attentive. "Now if you may be so kind, might I be allowed entry into your library to choose a book?"

"Oh," he said, beginning to stand up, "yes, of course."

"You need not trouble yourself, Charles," Mr. Darcy said suddenly as he entered the room. "I am more than willing to take your place and escort Miss Elizabeth to the library where she may choose her selection."

"Oh, thank you, Darcy. Miss Elizabeth, I believe Darcy shall do the job most credibly."

"Oh, but you need not trouble yourself either Mr. Darcy," Caroline said. "For I can ring for a servant to do the deed most credibly."

"It is no trouble, Miss Bingley."

She persisted. "Well, it is no trouble for me to escort you, because Miss Elizabeth, there is a particular book there that I do so adore, and I think that you shall like it. It is a conduct book that is most popular in my circles."

"Thank you for the offer, Miss Bingley, but I do not favor conduct books. There, you see," I said with a smile, "I am not a great reader."

As I left with Mr. Darcy, I glimpsed Caroline Bingley, and her eyes were like slits and her mouth set in a grim line.

As Mr. Darcy and I walked along the hall toward the library, I looked on him. "Why did you offer to walk me?"

"Because I felt compelled to."

"That was all?"

"No, I suppose not. I wished to speak with you."

"Should I have cause to worry about what we are speaking about?"

"Well, I shall not chew you up and spit you out."

"I should imagine not, for I would be hard to digest."

"I just wished to clarify."

"What?"

"That it is better that you should know me. I suppose that I can very well comprehend your affection for your sister, being an affectionate older brother myself."

"So, you are a good older brother then?"

"I want to believe so, though my past may speak differently for me."

"Oh, don't compare your conduct as a brother by your past. We all let our siblings down at some point. I just realized this but a short while ago myself."

"I cannot imagine you ever being anything less than affectionate toward Miss Bennet."

"Oh, thank you, and that was very kind. But it is not in that quarter. It is toward my other sister, Kitty, who I now see that I have been too quick to judge."

"Oh, your foolish sister."

"Mr. Darcy!"

"I meant no offense."

"And you gave it, nonetheless. I know that she merely appears as always chasing after Lydia, but I implore you to believe that there is more to her than that. It turns out that even I was in error. She has some fine qualities, some powers of discernment, and she is kind."

"But your sisters, if you may forgive me, are regarding a total want of propriety."

"She's in her teenage years," I said, "and she still has to grow up, that is all."

"I know women who are married at her age."

"And they are way too young for it," I demanded.

"Upon my word, Miss Elizabeth, you make a lot of declarations for so young a person. And such strange ones."

"Give it time, Mr. Darcy, and one day people shall learn that getting married at so young an age is detrimental and foolish in its own right. Tell me, did you know yourself in full at the age of seventeen?"

Mr. Darcy thought on this and was silent for a moment.

"No, you did not. You were expected to, and that was unfair, I know it. Well, as for us women, we do the same thing, do we not? We are expected to be full grown when we are full young, and then are chastised for suffering under the misconceptions of our age. I, sir, in my twenties, still admit to myself that I am not ready for marriage, and I know it now more than ever. Admit it; you are of the same mindset."

"You profess to know my mind, then?"

"I profess to thinking we are a little similar in that regard. Do you really think you are ready, at your age, for a wife?"

When I said this, his eyes darted toward me and then away.

"I cannot tell. In the brightness of the day, when in company, I enjoy the freedom that comes with being a single man, but in the coolness of night, I do so wish to have a wife."

When he spoke this, I faltered, surprised that he had allowed the conversation to take such a turn. Of course, since I had been used to blunter and brash statements in another time, I did not pretend to be shocked, for I was not.

"Did what I say unnerve you?" he asked. "My apologies."

"No, it did not."

"Really?" he asked as we walked along the bookshelves. "I am surprised."

"Your thought was a natural one, therefore who am I to nail you to a cross for it?"

He tilted his head to one side. "Yet you are right, I suppose. I am not ready for a wife."

"Because you are still wondering about the man you are. Well, I tell you, Mr. Darcy, that is a question that I have had many a time to myself, under the cover of night. I questioned if I was ready, and why I was not. And then I realized that I did not have to always have a reason for what I felt. I could and should just be allowed to feel. And it doesn't have to be pretty. Oh dear, am I talking too much?"

"Yes, quite so," he answered with a chuckle, to which I could not help myself but slap his shoulder, playfully. When I did this, he looked at the spot that I had touched, and I flinched.

"Oh, forgive me," I replied. "I forgot myself."

"No, you did not. That is just your way, is it not?"

I shrugged. "I suppose."

As I looked at the bookshelves, trying to find a book, I still saw Mr. Darcy looking at me.

"What?" I asked. "For it is quite rude to stare."

"What are you?" he asked simply.

"I beg your pardon?"

"What are you?"

"I am Elizabeth Bennet."

"Well, yes, but there is something else to it. It feels as if you are more than that."

I blushed and felt found out, but I immediately recovered. "I do not understand."

"You talk as if you love to determine the future, and that our present feels so obsolete to you, as if you are above everything."

"I do not possess foreknowledge, I can assure you, nor do I believe in witchcraft, sir. I merely love to believe the world will change one day."

He looked at me, raising an eyebrow as he did so. "And would you be heartbroken if it did not?"

"I do not have to be worried, for it's the world. And change is something that the world always loves to do!"

Mr. Darcy went to the bookshelves, found a book called 'Camilla,' and offered it to me.

"I do believe that you shall like this one."

"Did you like it?" I asked, taking it up and looking through it.

"My sister did."

"Then I shall render myself to her preferences."

"You should. My sister has good taste."

"She's a Darcy. I bet that was a prerequisite to being born."

Mr. Darcy smiled, despite himself. As I took the book, I stood before him. "Mr. Darcy, why did you really accompany me?"

"Because, I suppose, that I find you to be so very strange."

I winced. "Ouch, sir."

"Not in the horrid sort of way, but merely the different sort. I do not know what to make of you, or if I should even trust you. Yet the next moment, I feel myself wishing to always trust you."

"Mr. Darcy, even if you do not grow to like me, you can always trust me."

"I do not hate you, Miss Elizabeth. No, not at all. But when it comes to trusting you, that I have to choose for myself."

"Yes, I suppose that you do."

We were interrupted by Miss Bingley who entered.

"Oh, dear me," she exclaimed, "we were worried about where you had gone, so I was instructed to come and look for you both. You really quite scared us."

"Thank you, Miss Bingley, but I have my book now, the shelves did not eat us, and we may rejoin you all."

She looked a bit perplexed. "Ah, right."

With one last look, I left with Mr. Darcy and joined the family in the parlor.

When I returned with my book, Mr. Bingley, thinking the long time that we took in returning had to do with me not caring for his selection of books, began to offer his apologies.

"And I wish my collection were larger for your benefit and my own credit, but I am an idle fellow, and though I have not many, I have more than I ever looked into."

"And I can assure you that your selection suited me perfectly."

"I am astonished," Miss Bingley said, sitting down again, "that my father should have left so small a collection of books. What a delightful library you have at Pemberley, Mr. Darcy!"

"It ought to be good," he replied. "It has been the work of many generations."

"And then you have added so much to it yourself, you are always buying books."

"I cannot comprehend the neglect of a family library in such days as these," he answered.

"Neglect! I am sure you neglect nothing that can add to the beauties of that noble place. Charles, when you build *your* house, I wish it may be half as delightful as Pemberley."

Nodding, he said, "I wish it may."

"But I would really advise you to make your purchase in that neighborhood and take Pemberley for a kind of model. There is not a finer county in England than Derbyshire."

"To be sure," I said, in the midst of reading. "But Pemberly, from its location to its design and interior structure, is the very essence of architecture during Elizabethan England. While one can aspire to achieve such greatness a second time, it really ought not to be attempted, for such beauty cannot be established twice. Even the ballroom is rendered to rival the best room in London aristocracy. Even I, with my lack of caring for fancy houses and expensive homes, felt humbled when I saw it."

*Elizabeth, shut your mouth!*

But I told myself that too late, for all in the room looked at me as I spoke this. Mr. Darcy, who had been sitting down to compose a letter, had just turned to me.

"You have seen my home?" he asked.

I chewed my lip and decided that honesty was the best policy.

"Indeed, I have."

"I had not known this."

"Indeed," Mrs. Hurst remarked. "You have never mentioned it before."

"Because it was not a formal visit," I said, recalling my time in going with the future Mr. Darcy. "I had merely gone into Derbyshire to visit a friend, and we found ourselves befriending a tenant on the Pemberly estate, and he invited us to glimpse it from afar."

"But you spoke of my ballroom."

"Oh yes, my friend, she once knew a maid there, who told her of it, stating its regality. Yet when I had seen the place, I was quick to believe it," I fabricated quickly.

Mr. Darcy leaned back in his seat and looked on me more keenly.

"You liked my home?"

"Yes, I did indeed."

"Well, then you approve of it?"

"Yes, I daresay that there are few who would not approve."

"Yes, well, your opinion which is not often bestowed is more worth the…"

He trailed off as he looked around the room, then he removed his pen from the desk.

"I ought to begin composing this letter, for it shall not compose itself."

"Letters never do," I replied, and then I went back to my book.

Yet, while the discussion leant more toward Pemberly, I had to soon set my book down and listen, for they were all speaking of something that I thoroughly knew about, until Miss Bingley turned the discussion toward Mr. Darcy's letter.

"Who do you write to, sir?" she asked.

"I am writing to my sister."

"Oh, dear Georgiana! Is Miss Darcy much grown since the spring? Will she be as tall as I am?"

"I think she will. She is now about Miss Elizabeth Bennet's height, or rather taller."

When he said this, Miss Bingley and I looked on each other and then quickly looked away.

Miss Bingley said, "How I long to see her again! I never met with anybody who delighted me so much. Such a countenance, such manners! And so extremely accomplished for her age! Her performance on the pianoforte is exquisite. Do you play, Miss Elizabeth?"

"Yes, but very ill, indeed," I confessed.

"And that is the very word that is put to it often," Mr. Darcy spoke while he wrote. "I know many women who, when they are asked if they play, they only said 'yes, but very ill'."

"Are we to be set down for not being perfect?" I asked.

"No, you are only to be set down for undertaking that horrid task of pretending to be adequate at something that you quite excel in. It is modesty, but not the right sort."

"I cannot agree more," Miss Bingley supported. "Mr. Darcy, you have hit the nail right on the head when it comes to such things. There is nothing more deceptive than false modesty."

"And what if it is the truth?" I asked.

"It almost never is," Mr. Darcy insisted. "For I bet my life that you are quite a fine player at the pianoforte."

"And you flatter me after you doubt me. I am not stricken with false modesty when I say that I play poorly."

"We have a pianoforte there." Miss Bingley smirked. "And I should dearly love to hear you play it."

"Oh, but I…"

"No, I insist. We would love to hear you."

I bit my lip, looked at Mr. Darcy, who smiled, and I wanted to throw something at him.

As it came time for me to display my talents, I had no choice but to stand up and approach the pianoforte. I was not surprised this time when Mr. Darcy accompanied me to it to turn the pages.

"I have a simple piece that I know you shall like," he said.

"Mr. Darcy," I whispered, "what was the point of this?"

"Would you believe that I really just wished to hear you play?"

"Even though I am horrid, and you have made me open to the criticisms of women who cannot stand me already."

"I thought you were brave, Miss Elizabeth."

I smiled at him in disdain.

"Very well, Mr. Darcy, but do not be surprised if I step on your toes at some point in retaliation for this."

"Well, that is a very base reaction."

"You deserve it."

He opened the set of music and found a simple tune.

"Can you play this?"

"I do believe that I can."

In front of the whole company, I began to play the song, and then to my surprise, above me, Mr. Darcy began to sing the lyrics that were along with it. It was quite unprecedented, for I never would have known him to be the sort to sing, but he was. His voice was strong, baritone and deep.

I focused on my playing, but I had to take my time, pressed a couple of wrong keys, but overall, I was able to make it to the end of the piece. We were met by clapping which I knew was more for Mr. Darcy's singing voice rather than it was for my playing.

Miss Bingley was quick to praise him and forgot about me entirely as I sat down. To her dismay, as she got up to have her turn to play, Mr. Darcy offered to turn the pages for her but before doing so, he leaned close to me and I whispered to him.

"See I was not stricken by false modesty when I said that I played poorly," I voiced.

"But you played anyway."

I looked at him and smiled. "You have a lovely singing voice."

"Thank you."

He then went to Caroline Bingley and began to turn the music for her.

As they played, Mr. Bingley was kind and he sat down next to me. As Mr. Darcy turned Caroline's pages while she sang, Mr. Bingley leaned in close and whispered to me.

"I want to thank you, Miss Elizabeth."

"For what, sir?" I asked in reply.

"It is not very usual for my friend there to feel such comfort with a woman very quickly. And yet I see that he has quite taken to you so easily. It takes a rare sort of woman to gain his respect."

"Thank you, Mr. Bingley, but I have hardly gained his respect. We speak, and I do everything in my power to draw him out, but I daresay that he has only grown to tolerate me."

"I can assure you that it is a great deal more than that."

Surprised, I answered, "You think so?"

"Indeed, for when he speaks as much as he has spoken to you, it can only signify that he is quite comfortable, and that is an amazing thing."

"Thank you, Mr. Bingley."

"I find that the society of the country has quite pleased me."

"And therefore, it should only be lovely that your company being here has quite enhanced the joys of the neighborhood. I hope that, if you are the sort to have a love for town that it will not affect your plans to remain here. For our society has quite taken to your being here at Netherfield."

"And I have taken to them, I can assure you. For very quickly, the charms of the country have taken claims on my heart in ways that I did not foresee."

"That is how the best surprises always occur."

"Miss Elizabeth, please I need you to do me a favor."

"And what favor would that be?"

"I need you to—keep doing all in your power to make my friend over there comfortable. I know that he doesn't always give the best first impression, but that is all that it is; a bad first impression. Yet over time, his true nature arises, and he shows that he is a sturdy, loyal and dependable sort of man. And the way in which you draw him out, well, I have never heard him sing before."

"I never thought he could have!" I whispered even lower.

"Because he never shows that side of himself. I knew he could sing, but not that he ever would. But he only wants drawing out, that is all. And I want him to like it here."

"Because you like it here."

"Yes, and I quite depend on his good instruction."

"I understand all too well the desire to have that friend you rely on, and Mr. Darcy does the job credibly. He is sturdy, he is resourceful, and he cares for you deeply as a friend."

I turned to him. "Yet Mr. Bingley, when the time comes, I urge you to believe this: he can always advise you, but when it comes to matters of the heart, you always ought to guide yourself. Only you can determine your own happiness, and your judgment is your own. Nothing should shake it."

"Miss Elizabeth, why do you tell me this?"

"Because I know how hard it is to listen to your heart. Especially in the world that we live in. Therefore, I know that this is all presumptuous of me, but something tells me that you understand what I mean."

"Yes, I do of course," he replied, leaning back in his seat just as Caroline Bingley had finished playing and it was time to put the musical part of the evening to an end.

I hoped that I had done the right thing; I hoped that I had inspired both parties involved to just trust themselves. For, no matter the century, there were always too many voices from without trying to crack the soul and resolve of the person from within.

# Chapter Nine

## THE ACCIDENT

The next day, I awoke, went down to breakfast and to my surprise, all were present except for Mr. Darcy. Even Jane was sitting down and eating in the company. Once I arrived and took my seat, I inquired as to where Mr. Darcy was.

"He woke with an inclination for an early morning ride," Caroline Bingley said. "Surely Miss Elizabeth, you do not need to worry about his whereabouts, do you?"

I was about to open my mouth to give a gentle defense, when to my surprise, Jane spoke up for me.

"My sister merely spoke out of concern," Jane answered sweetly. "For she knows how much Mr. Darcy means to your company and would not wish for anything to befall you all here."

"Precisely," Mr. Bingley also stressed. "And that is very good of you."

"I thank you both," I said, gave a quick glance at Caroline who looked as if she had gotten slapped across the face, and then I eased my way into the company.

Yet as I ate, there was a strange sense in my stomach, as if there was a foreboding of some kind. As I searched my brain to recall what it was that could have unnerved me, only then did I realize what I was looking for.

In the future, Mr. Darcy was known for having disappeared suddenly. Yes, this could have been a simple mid-morning ride, but it also could have been something more. Why was he taking so long?

Therefore, I ate my breakfast quickly, and then wondered how best to excuse myself from the table. Therefore, I stood up and humbly requested if I might take a brief walk about the grounds, for I felt as if I had a headache of some kind.

Miss Bingley and Mrs. Hurst both gave each other a look, but Mr. Bingley allowed it. So, I retrieved my bonnet, and then left the house quickly. I found out from a maid where the stables were, went in the direction of them and found a stable hand cleaning a saddle. I asked him if he knew in what direction Mr. Darcy had gone, and he pointed east. At first, I had begun to walk away from him, but then I had the suspicion that I would not be enough. I told him that I worried that Mr. Darcy was in trouble, and if he would be so kind, would he ride out in the direction that he had gone, with me riding side-saddle behind him.

He agreed to this, and then we both rode off after Mr. Darcy. As we reached a couple of leagues away, we saw a black stallion, a magnificent beast, prancing around back and forth.

"Upon my honor!" the stable hand gasped.

"What?"

"That's Mr. Darcy's horse!"

"Can you race any faster?"

"Yes, I can."

He urged his horse onward and rushed along the land at full speed while I had to hold onto the ribbons of my bonnet for fear of it blowing off. Very soon we came upon the horse; he climbed down, calmed the horse and looked around.

"Where is he?"

Next to the horse, there was a small stream, and my eyes scanned around, seeing no sign of Mr. Darcy until I realized something.

"Oh my god!" I jumped down from the horse and rushed forward.

"Miss?" The stable hand inquired.

"The water! He fell into the water!"

Without bothering to care about anything else but him, I rushed into the stream and began to search around and then I saw Mr. Darcy's body lying at the bottom. When he fell, he must have knocked his head against something and was unconscious. Now he was drowning.

I raced up to him, leaned down and pulled his head and shoulders out of the water.

"Help me!" I cried to the stable hand.

"Right." He rushed up to me and together we carried Mr. Darcy's body out of the water and lowered him to the ground nearby.

We laid him down, and I rested my ear against his chest.

"I can't hear a heartbeat."

The stable hand pressed his hand against Darcy's nose.

"I'm sorry, but he's not breathing. He's dead, Miss."

"No, he's not," I shouted. "He just has too much water in his lungs. That's all! That's all!"

I opened up his jacket and vest, then rubbed my hands, and thanked god that we had to learn CPR to be certified babysitters in the agency that I was a part of in 2016, because now I would have to put it to good use. With determination I kissed him to give him mouth to mouth resuscitation, and then I began to pump his chest to get his heart moving. I breathed air into his lungs again, then pumped, still nothing.

I repeated the action.

Still nothing.

No, he would not die!

I promised his descendant so very faithfully. I could not let that Mr. Darcy down.

I had loved him! I had wanted him! And now there was no way that I could ever return to the future to have him! The least I could have was the victory of holding to the promise that I gave him. This was all that I had left. No love, no hope, just this!

I was Elizabeth Bennet, the girl who had fallen through time. Through space. And then returned, there and back again. Moment by moment, I had fallen and risen again. I was lost and then I found my way in the forest of the unknown, I had watched a man I loved meet another woman at the altar, marry her, and then I still clapped for him.

I faced knowing that my parents might be lost to me forever, my sisters! I watched as time ran out for them, when I had discovered that they had died long ago, that they were released into the unknown, and there was nothing of us left, no Jane, no Kitty, no Mary or Lydia —just me.

I had walked in worlds where the horse was replaced by a metal machine that had run on gas! I had watched time fold over on itself and give way to airplanes, trains and even the spaceship! I had watched the moon landing on a device that no one would believe would exist one day, in the year of 1969.

I saw humanity stretch itself to the breaking point, and still not break.

I had learned that we overcame injustice, that women could vote, that slavery had ended, that war was still the world's way, and now here I was, not saving the one life that I could. But no, if I could do all those things, and still survive, I could do this! I could do this!

I will save Mr. Darcy! And he will live!

I pressed my hands on his heart once more after pumping air into his lungs.

He would live!

He would—

With a huge outbreath, Mr. Darcy's chest rose up and down and he gasped out for air.

"He's alive!" I screamed, almost crying. "He's alive."

"Oh blimey," the stable hand gasped. "How in the bloody hell did you do that?"

"CPR," I replied.

"Oh. What?"

"Never mind that. We have to get him to the house, so please help me get him onto the horse."

"Can you ride at all?"

"Not really."

"My horse can hold two, but it can't hold three."

Coming to a decision, I went over to Mr. Darcy's horse, pulled him toward the stable hand and asked if he could hold Mr. Darcy's form while also attaching my horse's reins to his horse's saddle at all.

The stable hand unbound the horse's reins to make them longer so that he could hold it around his arm and Mr. Darcy securely in front of him. I mounted the other horse, not side-saddle, held on to dear life, while the stable hand rode us back to Netherfield Park.

Once we reached the entrance of the house, someone must have seen us from a window, because very soon, Mr. Bingley, the Hursts and Miss Bingley, were rushing from out of the house and up to us.

"Darcy!" Mr. Bingley cried. "What has happened?!"

"He fell from his horse, into the stream on the estate, and almost died from drowning," I reported quickly. "We must get him inside and get a doctor quickly."

"Of course," Miss Bingley said, stressed. "Oh, we must get him in of course!"

"I just said that!" I bellowed, at my wit's end. I jumped down from my horse.

"And what are you doing riding like a man!" Caroline hissed.

"Caroline, there are more pressing issues," Mr. Hurst said, as he, Mr. Bingley and I lowered Mr. Darcy's unconscious form from the stable hand. I thanked him and then we carried Mr. Darcy up the steps and into the house.

"How did this happen?" Mrs. Hurst kept asking. "How did this ever happen?"

# Chapter Ten

## JUST TO HEAR HIM BREATHING

M r. Darcy was taken to his room where some servants tended to him, and Jane and I waited in seats outside of his room after I had changed my clothes. Eventually the apothecary came to tend to him. Finally, after some assistance, he determined that Mr. Darcy was well, but had suffered from a concussion. Also, he had administered stitches, then bandaged Mr. Darcy's head from where he had fallen and split his head open.

After what had felt like forever, Jane and I were told that Mr. Darcy had opened his eyes at last. Mr. Bingley had exited and allowed us entry as well as sending for the stable hand who had helped me save his life.

When we had entered, Miss Bingley and Mrs. Hurst were already there, and they were standing near his bed as Mr. Darcy's eyes fell upon me.

"Mr. Darcy!" I gasped. "Oh, I am so very happy to see you awake, sir!"

He gave me a lazy smile. "It is nice to be awake."

"Yes, we were ever so worried about you," Jane stressed.

"And do you remember anything?" I asked. "Anything of what happened?"

"For goodness sakes, Miss Elizabeth," Caroline reprimanded. "He has just had a fall, and he need not be questioned at this time."

"Yes," I replied, very much not wishing to hold my tongue. "Forgive me, I was being insensitive."

"Yes, you were, my dear. Mr. Darcy has just had a tragic accident."

"Yes, he has, for I was there to find him."

"You what?" Mr. Darcy asked suddenly.

"Well yes, I…" I turned to Miss Bingley. "What was he told?"

We were interrupted when the door to Mr. Darcy's room opened and the stable hand entered, followed by Mr. Bingley and Mr. Hurst.

"How is he doing, then?" the stable hand asked, and then he saw that Mr. Darcy's eyes were open. "Oh, very good, sir. You're a lucky lad, aren't you? This woman got to you just in time."

When the stable hand pointed to me, Mr. Darcy's eyes darted from me to Caroline.

"You said it was the stable hand who saved me," Mr. Darcy remarked.

"Well, I thought it was so," she replied. "He was the one bringing you on his horse."

"Miss Bingley," I replied, diplomatically, "I can very well comprehend how you were mistaken on that score."

"What was I to be mistaken about?"

"Mr. Watson here told me something very different," Mr. Bingley said, gesturing to the stable hand.

"What occurred to me, sir?" Mr. Darcy asked the man named Watson.

"Oh, well," Watson said, "a little while after you had left for a morning ride, Miss Elizabeth here came to the stables, believing that something might have befallen you. Therefore, she asked if I would take her in the direction of where you had ridden, sir. I took her, and we found your horse pacing about, looking nervous, and then Miss Elizabeth here guessed that you may have fallen into the stream, and then she rushed in to find you. She did, then we pulled you out of the water and…"

As Mr. Watson continued to narrate the history of what had occurred, I then began to put the pieces together. That was why Mr. Darcy had quite disappeared from all records possibly. The other Mr. Darcy had said that his history faded soon after he had come, but it must have been a little after. He had been riding along the grounds; he had ridden into the water, either his horse faltered, or Darcy just fell.

When he did, he fell into the water, his head must've hit something, rendering him unconscious and then he drowned. It was even more likely that his corpse would have floated downstream as well, and they never would have known what happened to him. Yet now it didn't happen. Was that why I was not allowed to remain in 2016 with the Mr. Darcy that I had fallen in love with? Because of his ancestor?

He needed someone to know what had happened to him; therefore, they would be the only ones who would be able to stop it from happening. Now, time would be moving in a different direction. Because of this, would time change? Would the Mr. Darcy I had met even be born? Of course, he ought to be, because he came from a different branch of the family that was closely connected, but then again...all it took was one domino to fall in a different direction for anything to change. And would he have inherited Pemberly?

Time really was quite complicated.

Yet I could not think of it now, for Mr. Watson had just finished his narration and all in the room turned to me.

"But if I was dead," Mr. Darcy said, "how did you save me?"

"Oh, it's called cardiopulmonary resuscitation," I said. "I pressed my hand against your chest to get your heart beating and then breathed air into your lungs from my mouth."

All in the room blinked other than Mr. Watson.

"It was all innocent," Mr. Watson assured them, "and it quite saved his life, you see."

"How exactly did you breathe air into his lungs?" the apothecary asked me.

"I pressed my lips against his and gave him my air," I confessed. When I announced this, Caroline Bingley covered her mouth.

"You did such a thing!" She gasped. "That is vulgar and base!"

"It saved his life!" I replied.

"It did, Miss Bingley," Mr. Watson replied. "It really did revive him."

"Miss Bingley, when you drown, water fills your lungs," I instructed, "and the only thing to counteract this is to breathe air into a person's lungs, push out the water and get the heart beating again."

"I have never heard of such a practice," the apothecary said.

"Oh, it is popular amongst sailors on ships," I lied. In truth, I had no idea if sailors in my time knew of it or not. Yet since the British Navy was not present to contradict me, I believed I was quite safe from any objections.

"Oh, of course they would know," the apothecary believed. "Yes, I can see the logic of that."

"I had no idea you even knew any sailors, Lizzy." Jane gave me a small smile. "Oh, thank goodness you came to Netherfield when you did."

Mr Bingley agreed. "Yes, indeed, for I owe you much, Miss Elizabeth. You saved my friend."

"It was my pleasure," I said, and then we all turned to Mr. Darcy.

"You really saved my life?" he whispered, looking humbled.

"The effects of being a great walker, I suppose. We are not afraid of walking towards things. And you are very welcome."

After the apothecary declared that Mr. Darcy would recover fine in the course of a few days, he still recommended him to stay in bed for three days, and after many kind words spoken by Miss Bingley, he was informed that he ought to rest, to which we all left him alone.

As we did, I breathed out a sigh of relief. Mr. Darcy was saved, just to hear him breathing was music to my ears, I had completed my mission, and when the time came, I could go home, and be glad and at peace.

# Chapter Eleven

## CLANDESTINE CONVERSATIONS

J ane once more returned to her room to remain in bed for a time.

"What a turn of events, I declare!" She got into her nightgown and crawled under the covers. "Poor Mr. Darcy. Here I am, in bed from a cold, finding myself to be unfortunate, when he almost died if not for you."

"Yes, fortune was with him."

"My dear Lizzy." She smiled and took my hand. "You really were a godsend to us both. If you had not come and tended to me, then who knows what would have happened? I have no idea at all what would have occurred, and I do not wish to, for it is too painful to think of. And to think, that now Mr. Darcy quite owes you his life."

"Yes, I suppose that he does."

She gave me a sly smile. "I do believe that he shall admire you now."

I gave her a poignant look. "Or feel insecure around me."

"No, Lizzy, I am sure that you are wrong. He is not that sort of man. He will revere you now, as you deserve. Thank you, Lizzy."

"You are welcome of course."

"No, not for that. Because of the advice that you gave me from Charlotte Lucas. You both were correct, I should have showed my feelings a little more, and helped him on. I did not before, and I realize now that there is nothing wrong with sometimes showing what we feel. If not, then there is no way that we can ever gain what we aspire to. Oh dear, am I evil for thinking of that now when Mr. Darcy has had such a bad episode?"

I laughed and assured her that she was not evil at all and her serenity was returned back to its proper place.

As we spoke, there was a knock on the door, and I went to open it to find a servant who looked at me kindly.

"Miss Elizabeth," she whispered, "I was sent to give you this under the express desire that you do not mention it."

"Thank you." I took it, opened it as she left, but not in the room with Jane. Therefore, quite alone in the hall, I perused its contents.

*Dear Miss Elizabeth,*

*If you do not mind, I wish to speak with you. This may be very indelicate to ask, but I know that you are not the sort to take offense to my pleas. I shall be alone in my room for this next hour, and I wish to be acquainted with your story of how you found me. If you would please come with haste, I would be glad of it. And you need have no fear of committing any breach in propriety, for my valet, Mr. Harrison, shall be in attendance the entire time, therefore you shall not be alone. Please, for my peace of mind, visit me now so that we may speak in each other's confidence.*

*F. Darcy*

I closed the letter and came to a decision quickly; for indeed, I did owe him that much.

I went into the room and told Jane that I would return soon, and then left to see Mr. Darcy.

When I reached his room, the door was opened, and the man named Mr. Harrison greeted me. He spoke to me kindly, and then when I entered, there was a maid there as well who was on good terms with Mr. Harrison, in order to see to it that I was not alone in the room. However, when I walked in, the room being a spacious one offered me the ability to speak silently with Mr. Darcy while they remained on the other side of the room, giving us our privacy.

As I entered, Mr. Darcy was in bed, propped up on his pillows and he looked at me boldly when I sat down in a chair next to his bed.

"How are you feeling?" I asked.

"Alive, and I suppose that is a great feeling."

"Well, it's nice to see that your personality has not altered in any way," I joked.

"I suppose it is my way, that in the face of tragedy, I know not how to pass it off as more than a joke."

"I do not know if I recommend that thought process or shun it. I must consider further on the morrow if you are very wise for doing so, or very foolish."

"You joke."

I gave him a soft gaze. "I was not the one who almost lost his life."

"No, you are merely the one who saved it."

When he said this, I faltered and looked down.

"Have I silenced you?" he asked innocently. "Dear me, that was not my intent."

"Then what is your intent? Why did you send for me?"

He held my gaze. "Why did you come?"

"Are you really in earnest?"

"Yes."

I released a sigh. "My question is a perfectly logical one, given the circumstances. Yours is, well, I cannot fully say what yours really is."

"I just worried that you would not come."

"We are not fully breaching propriety, because we do nothing untoward. We are in company now and I am safe. And we did really need to talk, I suppose. And without the critical eyes of those two harpies."

"And by that remark, I am assuming that you mean Miss Bingley and Mrs. Hurst."

"I am not afraid to reveal to you what I feel toward them. Something tells me that you shall not go and begin to start whispering my words to them."

"No, I will not. Especially since, if there is any justice in the world, they have not been particularly kind toward you."

"No, they have not. But can you tell me, why are they my enemies? I have done nothing to them."

"You truly don't know your own sex? You all view each other as each other's competition."

I gave him a steady glance. "You presume to know much about my species."

He gave me a satisfied look. "I speak as I find."

"And you paint a very bad portrait of us."

"I speak as I find," he repeated.

"Be careful, or I shall be forced to say what I determine about you."

"You cannot do that."

"And why not?" I asked.

"Because you saved my life."

"And how does that keep me from criticizing you?"

"It means that you, to some extent, are responsible for me."

When Mr. Darcy made that remark, I gasped, but in some strange light, it did make some sense.

"I can see why your mind would think that I owe you that, but since I saved your life, you owe me something at the very least."

"And what is that?"

"You owe me an answer. Why did you send for me?"

"Because I wish to be able to thank you on my own terms."

Mr. Darcy raised his arm toward me for me to take. I leaned forward and took his hand in my own.

"Miss Elizabeth Bennet," he said. "Thank you so much for saving my life, and I owe you much. I owe you all."

He leaned forward and kissed my hand, and exceedingly flattered, I felt heat creep up my neck.

"Well, you are very welcome, Mr. Darcy, and you make me blush."

"I am happy that I do."

"Well," I said lightly, sitting down again. "You must make sure to take it quite easy for the next few days. For if your head is damaged, then you shall have dizzy spells throughout the day, and you must do all in your power to prevent that."

"I shall do so," he replied. "Even the apothecary has recommended such."

"Also, you must make sure to keep cold and also hot rags on your head as well, and I know that you shall change your head bandages every now and again when they get dirty."

His smile was warm, and his eyes twinkled. "You are quite the nurse, then?"

"If you do not mind. And since you feel as if I am responsible for you, then might I request staying for a few more days, until I feel that you have quite recovered? I can tend to you and Jane, and if you were to ask it of Mr. Bingley, then he shall accept it."

At my request, Mr. Darcy's eyes gleamed. "You wish to do so?"

"This way I can guarantee that you are well, and that you shall look after yourself. I know that you have the best of service here, but I simply wish to oversee you till all is well. Jane will soon be on the mend, but I am certain that Mr. Bingley would not care if she remained even after she was well."

"No, he would not."

"Would you mind it?"

"No, I very much would not. Miss Bennet, I have had Mr. Harrison write for me to my sister, who will come to Netherfield perhaps, since I have had this accident. When she comes, would you meet her?"

His request pleased me. "Well, if you desire it, then I would be willing to meet her."

"I must warn you, she is a bit shy."

"Much like her brother when I met him?" I asked archly, and he smiled briefly.

"Yes, she and I do have that in common."

"It is a natural habit."

"Yes, it is, I suppose. And I shall ask Mr. Bingley once you leave."

"Very good."

"Miss Elizabeth, there is something else that I must ask."

"You may."

"Mr. Watson said that you assumed that I was in danger. What made you assume such?"

"It was just a…gut feeling, if that is the proper term for it."

"I understand your meaning. You just assumed that I could be hurt."

"Yes, for you had been taking so long of a time."

"Well, whatever voice that you have within you that spoke of this, I am happy for it."

I gave him a warm smile. "We both are."

I stood up and was about to excuse myself. As I went to the door to leave, Mr. Darcy called to me.

"Miss Elizabeth, I have one more question."

"Yes?"

"Why did you do this? Even if you had a gut feeling as you phrased it, what sparked you to act on it?"

"Well, I suppose that your face is most amusing when you smile, so there."

"But I rarely ever smile."

"True."

"So, what is the real reason?"

"Well, it is simple."

"How simple?"

"Very simple."

"Then tell me."

"Well, I suppose, it is because we are friends. And I look on us as such."

He cocked his head. "Do you?"

"Yes."

I curtsied to him and then left the room, making sure to keep our clandestine conversation brief.

# Chapter Twelve

### TIME VERSUS FATE

Mr. Bingley was very eager to have us stay, much to the chagrin of Miss Bingley and Mrs. Hurst, and the indifferent attitude of Mr. Hurst. Even when Jane recovered, we still did not leave the estate, which was good for her chances with Mr. Bingley, who was quickly growing enamored with her, especially since she was making it innocently clear that she was quite taken with him.

Our mother, in hearing that our stay was prolonged, could not have been happier, and our sisters even visited us at Netherfield to escort them into Meryton. While they had come in our carriage, they asked the Bingley sisters if they would like to attend, but they claimed to desire a day in to get 'work' accomplished. Therefore, we were allowed to go alone. However, before leaving, Mr. Bingley asked if Lydia was prepared to name the day of the ball, as she heard him speak of holding one, and she had made her decision. Therefore, with his general goodness, he sent her away content that she had gotten the idea of a ball into his head.

Before leaving, I verified that Mr. Darcy was going to remain in the house for the duration, and even as we left, I saw him glimpse down at us from his window. I waved to him and then set off for our outing.

"Oh, since you two have been away playing nurse and invalid," Lydia said, "we have been enjoying the delights of our new acquaintances. Always we are seeing officers nearly every day. And some fancy me, I declare. Do they not, Kitty?"

"It's hard to tell, you know," Kitty replied, "but I do wish that I had 20,000 pounds to my name, and therefore all of the soldiers would be violently in love with me."

"I'm sure that they would be in love with me first!" Lydia declared.

"And I am sure that they would be in love with me."

"No, they would love me more!"

"No, they would love me more!"

"Oh, for god sakes, you both," I proclaimed. "Who cares who they would prefer? Unless you desire men to marry you for your money and nothing more, then I don't think either of you would fancy the match you make."

"All I ask is that a man looks nice in regimentals," Lydia declared, "and care for nothing else."

"Lydia, you will learn to care for more in the end," Jane assured her. "Depend on it."

⬥

As we journeyed into Meryton, we were looking at a bonnet in a shop's window, when Lydia noticed some officers that she had met before.

"Oh, look! Kitty, there is Denny and Captain Carter!"

"Oh, Lizzy and Jane," Kitty said. "Yes, those are two particular gentlemen who we have met a lot. I think Denny is the handsomer of the two, but Lydia is stupid and thinks Carter is."

"You are the stupid one."

"Am not, oh but who is that next to them?"

We all looked and there I noticed the man I had met a short while ago, when the officers had come into town.

"Mr. Wickham," I whispered aloud.

"You know him, Lizzy?" Jane asked.

"Well, not really. I merely met him by accident when the officers had first come into town."

"Lizzy," Kitty asked, "you recall him well. Is he not mightily good-looking though?"

"I admit, he is quite handsome in feature, but he is not to my taste."

She laughed at that. "I do not believe you. For he is quite comely, and from last I recall, he suited your tastes a great deal."

"Quiet now, for they are looking upon us."

"Denny and Carter!" Lydia cried, waving to them for all to notice.

"Lydia, please…" Jane sighed. "Do not make us into such a spectacle."

"Oh, Jane, don't be such a fussy one about it."

Denny, Carter, and the man Mr. Wickham came over and we met them all. Denny and Carter were quite pleasant gentlemen, and they met us gracefully.

"Miss Bennet and Miss Elizabeth," Denny said, "we have heard much of you both and the praises that are attached to your names are quite fitting."

"Ah, it is always frightful to hear that one is spoken of," I allowed, "but if the words be kind, then I always welcome the report."

"As you should," Captain Carter added.

"And might we introduce you to our friend," Denny said. "Mr. George Wickham."

"Ladies," Mr. Wickham said, bowing to us, and producing a smile as handsome as his features. "I am quite delighted to make your acquaintance, for the five sisters of Longbourn are quite the local legend."

"We always attempt to be nothing less," Lydia boasted.

"There Lizzy," Kitty said, "you were right, his name is Wickham."

I gave Kitty a look, and Mr. Wickham turned to me, his kind eyes showing much gentleness.

"Ah, yes, we have met slightly have we not?" he remarked.

"Yes, ever so slightly. Just enough to say it was so, but never enough to say it was much."

"May that be remedied," he replied.

"I do believe that it already is. Do you plan to stay long here in Hertfordshire and Meryton, Mr. Wickham?"

"All the winter, I am happy to say. For I have taken up a post in the regiment, and therefore shall begin active employment in serving my country."

"Ah, then we shall see you in regimentals soon, I dare say," Lydia answered.

"If that is your pleasure, Miss Lydia, then yes you shall."

"We were just walking about in hopes of seeking a new bonnet," Kitty reported.

"Well then," Carter suggested, "are you in need of company, or for the rugged taste of us soldiers to give their suggestions?"

"We would love that, for we had great hopes of encountering you," Lydia acknowledged before any of us could stop her. Denny was joined by Kitty and Jane, Lydia dominated the attention of Carter, and therefore I was left to stand near Mr. Wickham as we followed the rest.

"Do not worry," I said, "this time I promise that I shall not drop anything and leave you forced to pick it up."

He smiled, showing strong teeth. "A great pity for it then. For I quite liked having the position of picking up the things that have the foolishness to get away from you."

I blushed as we entered the shop.

Since I had no real need for a bonnet, I did not have the impulse to look around, but of course, all it took was one ribbon woven in an interesting way along the straw of the bonnet for me to get curious, and all the while, while I inspected a certain piece, Mr. Wickham stayed at my elbow.

"I must confess that I shall be of little help," he admitted, "for I am by no means proficient in telling a lovely bonnet from a horrid one."

"Then you are not alone and may offer company to all the other members of your gender who have been stricken with such a fate," I offered. "Also, if it makes you feel any more confident about yourself, I know many a woman who prides herself on being able to tell a good bonnet, when it is in fact quite gruesome to the eye."

Mr. Wickham laughed at this.

"Yes, even we women can be quite horrid in our taste."

"Then I ought not to feel alone."

"No, you ought not to."

When he smiled at me once more, I could not help but feel slightly uneasy in my stomach. He was a man with much to recommend him, from his looks to his manners, and very soon, I felt a comfort in his presence. It was a comfort that I had not felt with a man since Mr. Darcy of the 21$^{st}$ century. Yet therein lay the problem. Should I abandon all hope of ever seeing him again fully? We were separated by time, and to be fair, he never said that he had loved me at all, so what was I holding on to?

Nothing!

Just a dream, I suppose.

Therefore, perhaps it was time I let the memory of him go at last, live in the moments of the present, and allow myself to feel. Yes, perhaps it was time to move on and keep going, as one ought to do.

Turning to Mr. Wickham, I wondered, what harm could there have been simply with me finding him agreeable? These were questions with quite a simple answer actually.

"So, you are joining the militia," I continued.

"Yes, and I suppose that I find my fortune to be quite great. I am well acquainted with some of the men already, as you have seen, and they are pleasant and congenial company. I find that I shall be placed in a society that is as agreeable as any I could have imagined. Also, I am of the active sort, and I cannot bear to be idle."

"I know the nature. To be born with roaming feet."

"Am I to believe that our natures are more similar than different?"

"I give you time to get to know me better, Mr. Wickham, and if you like my nature, then you may compare it to yours. However, if you find me to be a wild beast, or a bitter crow, you may not wish to compare us."

His smile was warm. "I could never think such of you, I believe, for your nature is clear from the first."

"Is it? Well, should I be worried that my nature is so easy to determine?"

"Never, there is something to be said for those who appear as quite artless. Also, what is there to be so smart about having a complicated nature? It is not better than a simple one."

"Do you define me now, or do you define yourself?"

"I defined myself and I hope to define you in the process."

"Well, time will tell if you are right in the end. Though we must be careful."

"And why is that?" he asked.

"Because time has sometimes proven, in my experience, to be a tricky thing when having one see things clearly."

"Then maybe we should not leave it up to time."

"What should we leave it up to?"

"Fate."

I waggled a finger at him. "Oh, but she can be an even trickier beast."

He tilted his head toward me. "Can she?"

"Yes," I joked. "I would know. For I've met her."

"Have you?" He smiled. "Pray tell me, what was she like?"

"Very changeable…and indecisive."

Eventually we had finished our shopping trip, in which Kitty bought a simple bonnet that she was going to dress up herself, and Lydia bought a vile bonnet, only because there were five uglier ones in the shop. Yes, that was her logic.

Eventually we parted ways with the officers and Mr. Wickham gave me one last furtive look of flirtation.

"I can see into your mind," Kitty said.

"Can you?"

"Yes, and you lied. You think him handsome."

"Very well. Only a mere little."

"I knew it!"

"Oh, good for you."

# Chapter Thirteen

## THE LETTER

W e then took the carriage to Longbourn to see our parents before we were to return to Netherfield Park, and when there, we were graced with some interesting and unpleasant news.

"I hope, my dear," our father said to our mother as we were sitting down to our mid-day meal, "that you have ordered a good dinner today, because I have reason to expect an addition to our family party."

"Who do you mean, my dear?" she asked, for he had quite interrupted her when she was asking us of how our time in Netherfield was progressing. "I know of nobody that is coming, I am sure, unless Charlotte Lucas should happen to call in and I hope *my* dinners are good enough for her.

"I do not believe she often sees such at home. But then it wouldn't be her, for she would only come for Lizzy, and Lizzy is quite at Netherfield."

She turned to me. "And while I wondered that you would go, Lizzy, for there was nothing for you at Netherfield, now I am quite happy for it. My daughter was the one to save Mr. Darcy! Oh, you have done such a good thing for Jane. After all, by saving him, naturally it would endear Jane to Mr. Bingley more, for she appears as a saint just by association."

"Yes, Mama, when I was saving Mr. Darcy's life, of it being an advantage to my sister was the chief motive for my actions."

"Of course, it was, Lizzy," our father noted, "but the person of whom I speak is a gentleman, and a stranger."

"Is it Mr. Bingley? Oh, pray, I hope it is Mr. Bingley and not someone that I detest!"

"Oh, my dear, I am so very sorry for you, but it is someone that you do quite detest. It is *not* Mr. Bingley. It is a person whom I never saw in the whole course of my life."

She fanned herself with her handkerchief. "Oh, do not leave us in suspense, Mr. Bennet, for you know how much I hate it when you leave me in suspense."

"And I love doing it, but here it is," he said, taking out a letter from his pocket. "About a month ago I received this letter, and about a fortnight ago I answered it, for I thought it a case of some delicacy, and requiring early attention. It is from my cousin, Mr. Collins, who, when I am dead, may turn you all out of this house as soon as he pleases."

Our mother grew anxious. "Oh! I cannot bear to hear that name mentioned. Pray do not talk of that odious man. I do think it is the hardest thing in the world, that your estate should be entailed away from your own children."

"Yes, that is a crime that Mr. Collins was born committing, even before he knew what a crime was. But if you will listen to his letter, you may perhaps be a little softened by his manner of expressing himself."

Our mother's nose went in the air. "I have hated him too long to be able to stop now, I fear. I think it is very impertinent of him to write to you at all, and very hypocritical. I hate such false friends. Why could he not keep on quarreling with you, as his father did before him?"

"Because life can never be so simple as that, you see, because in England, every now and again, we stumble on the revolutionary idea of allowing peace to enter our lives. Now here, I shall read, and I am happy that Lizzy and Jane, you are come back to hear it."

*Dear Sir,*

*The disagreement subsisting between yourself and my late honored father always gave me much uneasiness, and since I have had the misfortune to lose him, I have frequently wished to heal the breach, but for some time I was kept back by my own doubts, fearing lest it might seem disrespectful to his memory for me to be on good terms with anyone with whom it had always pleased him to be at variance.*

*My mind, however, is now made up on the subject, for having received ordination at Easter, I have been so fortunate as to be distinguished by the patronage of the Right Honorable Lady Catherine de Bourgh, widow of Sir Lewis de Bourgh, whose bounty and beneficence has preferred me to the valuable rectory of this parish, where it shall be my earnest endeavor to demean myself with grateful respect towards her ladyship, and be ever ready to perform those rites and ceremonies which are instituted by the Church of England.*

*As a clergyman, moreover, I feel it my duty to promote and establish the blessing of peace in all families within the reach of my influence; and on these grounds I flatter myself that my present overtures are highly commendable, and that the circumstance of my being next in the entail of Longbourn estate will be kindly overlooked on your side, and not lead you to reject the offered olive-branch. I cannot be otherwise than concerned at being the means of injuring your amiable daughters, and beg leave to apologize for it, as well as to assure you of my readiness to make them every possible amends...*

The letter went on in this fashion, and then he had requested to be received at Longbourn on Monday of November 18th, by four o'clock and wished to remain for a fortnight.

"At four o'clock, therefore, we may expect this peace-making gentleman," our father said. "He seems to be a most conscientious and polite young man, upon my word, and I doubt not will prove a valuable acquaintance, especially if Lady Catherine should be so indulgent as to let him come to us again."

Our mother added, her spirit softening, "There is some sense in what he says about the girls, however, and if he is disposed to make them any amends, I shall not be the person to discourage him."

"Though it is difficult," Jane realized, "to guess in what way he can mean to make us the atonement he thinks our due, the wish is certainly to his credit."

"He seems to love his patroness, Lady Catherine de Bourgh a great deal, and I feel that he is a bit of an oddity," I noted, "for he apologizes for…"

I trailed off as I realized that this was the beginning of fate coming into action. Mr. Collins was coming to Hertfordshire to see us, and therefore, this was when and where he would meet Charlotte, they would fall in love and then get married. This was the beginning of that inevitability, and it frightened me.

"And he really is coming today?" I asked my father.

"Yes, he is."

"Well, I wish that we had spoken of this before," I replied, "for I wonder that maybe we needed more time being away from him. But now it is too late to send him away."

"Lizzy, you heard him yourself," Mary said, "and there was nothing but goodness, kindness and consideration in his address."

"Yes, I know, but what if it is too soon?"

"It cannot be," our mother replied, "for if he wishes to make amends to you all, then I shall not be the one to discourage him in any way. Now, Kitty, Lydia, Mary, and even you Lizzy, we must do everything in our power to make Mr. Collins feel drawn to us, to feel a connection that is both familiar and affectionate."

"Well, it shall not be me," Lydia cried, "for I could never marry a clergyman."

Our mother glared at her sternly. "Lydia, this is of vital importance."

"And what if he is not even handsome?"

"Find something else about him to like, then. Yet I desire this of you, to give the best first impression to Mr. Collins. Oh, to think, that if Mr. Bingley were to propose to Jane and Mr. Collins were to propose to one of you, then it would be perfect, and a double wedding too."

"Well, however we can be of assistance," Mary said. "It is always important to do one's duty. For being a clergyman is not a crime, but is quite a virtuous thing, for those who know how to appreciate the profession."

Lydia outwardly groaned at this, and Jane tried to chide her for it, but it was of no avail.

# Chapter Fourteen

## TWO STUBBORN MULES

Mr. Collins was not to arrive till after we left, therefore Jane and I were not to meet him, but instead were meant to very soon proceed to Netherfield. This was well enough, for with us being away, there still were the three remaining sisters. Also, with us being at Netherfield, our mother felt that it would show Mr. Collins how our family was establishing connections with the best society in the place.

Therefore, Jane and I proceeded to Netherfield Park once more, leaving Mary, Kitty and Lydia to be the ones to receive this 'oddity of a cousin' of ours. Yet when we returned to Netherfield, I was met by a very terrible sight that provoked me to no end. As we reached the entrance, Mr. Darcy was on his horse! Just riding along at a simple pace.

"I cannot believe him!" I blurted out to Jane. "He promised me that he would remain in bed. The devil lied to me."

"Lizzy, you cannot be angry with him," Jane pressed, "for I am certain that he does not wish to remain in bed forever."

"He almost drowned to death, Jane," I declared, turning on her with a fury. "You were not there. It was devastating."

"Elizabeth, are you learning to really care for him?"

"No, well, yes…but not in the way that you mean."

Once our carriage came to a halt, I jumped down, Mr. Darcy spotted us and began to ride toward us, but I ran towards him without any care for propriety and restraint.

I fought to catch my breath. "Mr. Darcy, what on earth do you do, sir? You are riding."

"Yes, well, I had the sudden urge to—"

"To break your word to me, sir? You promised that you would be in your room, and do not think that hard scowl of yours will frighten me. No, I shall not be deterred so. You could get hurt."

Mr. Darcy descended from his horse.

"Miss Elizabeth." He bowed his head. "I thank you for your worries, but you cannot order me around on this, and you are presumptuous to think otherwise."

"I am presumptuous?" I remarked, surprised at his tone.

"Yes, you are."

"And you are most ungrateful, you miserable sot!"

He was taken aback. "Did you just call me a—"

"Yes, I did. See? You do not frighten me. I just...you almost died, sir."

"I know that I did," he said, coming toward me. "Did you think that I had forgotten it?" His eyes were fierce and defensive.

"I cannot tell by your attitude," I replied. "Did you?"

"You offend me by saying so."

"You have quickly put yourself in danger so soon after you almost lost your life, and therefore you make my actions seem pointless, sir, and then your replies now only indicate a deeper flaw, does it not? A lack of gratitude or understanding for when one does something because one cares."

Turning my heel, I strode back to Jane.

"Fine then, sir, you may do as you like," I said over my shoulder, "for now I cease to care anymore. I've done my best. And you have not."

I walked up to Jane, took her arm and pulled her into the house.

"And you think that I like him," I whispered to her. "Jane, you must be joking."

Once we went in, we were met by Mr. Bingley, to whom I kindly excused myself as soon as I could, saying that I must get dressed for dinner, which he naturally agreed to, especially since it gave him a moment alone with Jane. Therefore, I went to my room and threw down my bonnet and cloak as I did so. Then I paced back and forth in frustration.

If I had saved the other Mr. Darcy's life in such a way, he would have understood my anger at his putting himself in harm's way. He would have understood my temper. However, like a moth to a flame, I had the impulse to walk towards the window and see if this Mr. Darcy was out there. When I did so, I saw him pacing around with his horse, pulling it by the reins, and then he stopped, his neck pricked up and it seemed as if he realized that maybe he might be observed.

He turned and looked at the house, his eyes scanned the windows and he saw me. When our eyes met, there was a bit of cold gravity behind our looks and we did not know what to do. Yet the way it is with all things, sometimes something can die as quickly as it could flare up.

In looking down at him, I began to comprehend that, despite having saved his life, I did not have control, nor should I have had control over his life. He was still his own lord and master. And of course, he could not keep himself under restraint and within doors. Naturally, he might have wished to roam about and continue on with his life. I did not like that he had lied to me, but I suppose it was well meant.

He stared up at me.

I stared down at him.

My eyes softened, and even if he couldn't see it from that distance, I hoped he would understand that I was no longer angry. Smiling apologetically, I waved down at him.

At first, he remained frozen, and then he raised his arm and returned the wave. I then pressed my hand against the glass, nodded and then moved away. Before doing so fully, I saw him turn around and lead his horse away to the stables.

To my surprise, as I was getting ready for dinner, changing into a gown that I needed no assistance in putting on, there was a knock on the door.

"Ah, is that you, Jane?"

"Miss Elizabeth?" Mr. Darcy voiced.

"Mr. Darcy?"

"Yes, I…are you quite willing to receive me just now?"

I went up to the door, opened it slightly and saw him through a crack in it.

"Well, I am quite ready for company, sir, but I do not wish for you to be convicted of any foul behavior by speaking with me through a door." I opened it and we stood, staring at each other.

"I know, but I just…I realized that I in fact did appear as being very ungrateful just then."

"Did you?"

"Yes, I did. I did promise that I would remain within, and when I did not, you must have thought that was me not caring to be sincere with you."

"Yes, I confess that I did feel that, and it hurt me. Yet if you are willing to be so candid, then I shall be so as well and tell you that while you confess to your shortcomings, I can reply in turn that I did not act at my best myself. I was not only quite short with you, but I was quite outrageous and overstepped my boundaries."

"Yes, I confess that the turn of your countenance when you hissed at me quite unnerved me."

"I suppose it did, and I was quite frightful, was I not?"

He gave me a small smile. "Yes, yes, you were."

Seeing him smile melted me somewhat inside, and for fear of him being observed by a gossiping servant, I exited my room and took his arm.

"Come; let us go to the music room so that we can talk further on the matter."

"Thank you, for we do quite need to discuss the matter further, don't we?"

I looked up at him. "Yes, we really ought to. After all, we are not so much two stubborn mules that we are willing to suffer the slings and arrows of miscommunication."

"We have not done so this far," he acknowledged, "therefore I hope that we do not do so at this point."

"No, I hope that we do not."

Eventually we reached the music room of Netherfield Park, entered it, and closed the door only slightly to give us a little bit of privacy but not fully. We sat down, with him in an armchair and me on a sofa.

First, we looked at each other.

I opened my mouth.

He opened his.

Then we began to speak at the same time.

Then I blushed and looked away.

"Pray continue," he offered.

"Nay, you may continue instead," I offered.

"Well…"

"Well…oh dear, now that we are here, I do not know how to begin." I began wringing my hands.

"Neither do I. Why does it feel as if fighting might have been an easier thing for us to do?"

"I do not know, but it does."

Agreeing, he answered, "Yes, it does."

"Yes, indeed it does."

Then to our utter surprise, we burst out laughing.

# Chapter Fifteen

## THE PROBLEM

Finally, after our laughter had subsided, we began to find our foothold in the conversation.

"What you must understand," I began, "when after saving one's life, one feels a little protective I suppose, and this sensation is so new that I did not know how to act upon it. But it is your fault as well, you know."

"And how so, do you figure this?" he asked archly.

"Well, you were the one who hinted at me being slightly responsible for you now, therefore it was really you that put the idea into my head, you see."

"Yes, I do confess that *that* part was a bit of my doing, I suppose. But in exchange for your admittance of your sudden outburst, I must also admit to my own fault in the matter. I did quite tell you that I was to remain indoors for the day, and I can suppose that, for you to come and see me prancing about on the very horse I fell from must have affected you."

"It seemed as if you did not care to keep your word."

"I just…it wasn't you. And I ought to have done as I promised, but you must understand, the truth about my nature, I refer to now."

He leaned forward. "Miss Elizabeth, I am not the sort who likes to be confined for very long in any situation. Nor do I like to remain indoors, unable to walk about, ride, and do as I will. I just… I despise being restrained, just as I do not feel that I can let this experience hold me down.

"Life brings risk to it, much risk, but just because one undergoes it doesn't mean that I just continue to hide from it. Such a practice is no way to live life."

"You're right," I gathered, "it's not, I suppose. But at least you could have prepared me for your action. And I do not mean to order your life in any way, but I merely wish for you to be frank and don't startle me in such a way."

I sighed heavily and looked away. "Really, *Mr.* Darcy, your intentions are noble, but from now on, you must mean what you say when it comes to me. And please, do not dare tell me that my input means nothing, for that would be very rude again."

"I should not have said that at all, for it was rude for one thing, and then untrue in the next," he pointed out. "I thank you for your concern, for it was your concern that saved my life. I owe you everything that I have, therefore, you have a right to care. And that you do care means a great deal to me."

"Does it?"

"Yes, it does. If you really do."

"Well, I suppose that I do, so don't be rude about it again, you must promise."

"I do."

"Very well," I said, extending my hand, "take hands with me and let us strike hands on the bargain."

Mr. Darcy took my hand and shook it.

"I do so like how quickly we resolved that argument," he commented.

"As do I, but you need never worry, for I spend much of my life attempting to never stay angry for long. Indeed, I suppose my personality could be viewed as swinging from one extreme to another in that way."

"It is not so, and you do yourself a disservice."

"Very well, I shall believe you. So, since you have found it within yourself to take up your seat on your horse again, how was it?"

"I know that you would think I was frightened, but it was so strange. I felt no such thing. He is a good horse, has always been wonderful, and it was an accident, no more and no less. Therefore, when I mounted him once more, I felt as if I still had all the comforts that I had on him before."

I nodded, understanding. "I suppose that it is wise, to not be afraid of life, for come what may."

"That does not mean that I do not appreciate what you did for me, for

I do. It is just that my nature is my nature, and I am quite resolute, always willing to go my own way."

"I know the feeling, for I can be quite determined, and I do not apologize for it."

He slapped his knee. "But I am being quite inconsiderate now, for I have not asked you anything about your day. Did you enjoy your trip into town and back to Longbourn?"

"I would have if it were not for the news that we had received when we were there."

"What news was this?"

I told Mr. Darcy all about the arrival of Mr. Collins and how Longbourn was entailed away from our family and was his to inherit. When I finished my narration, Mr. Darcy summed up my report.

"So then the fate of your family is that of a common one; you lose the house to an outside male heir, and now, as the only proscription that your mother can find, is for one of your sisters to bind herself to him."

"It is the only way that we can keep the estate. Therefore, one of us must suit his fancy."

"Surely you are not thinking of yourself in this case, are you?" he retorted. "You are not planning on considering this man that you have never met?"

"No, indeed. I am not the sort to do as I am expected when it is not a duty that I agree with. Unless I were to meet him and were to fall in love with him, I would not choose him."

"Good. Too often I have seen the scraping of advantageous matches in this world, and no affection in the case. It is a dismal business."

"A very dismal one. Unfortunately, such occurrences happen more often than not."

"Precisely. Miss Elizabeth, I must apologize about something."

I raised my eyebrows and gave him a sly smile. "What sin have you committed of late?"

"I must apologize for disbelieving your sister as not being suitable for my friend. She is a very lovely sort of woman, with a gentle disposition, and now it is clearer, so my first impediment for the match has quite been lifted."

"What was your last reason for thinking her not perfect for him?"

"It was not what you think."

"I think nothing, so tell me."

"I thought that she didn't care for him."

"I beg your pardon?"

"Yes, your sister's personality, her spirit and character always appeared to be a restrained one, a serene one. And the serenity of her countenance always left something wanting, for it appeared that while she found Mr. Bingley's attentions toward her pleasing, but there was no affection from her. To be frank, she just seemed to only like him, and not love him, and it appeared as if her heart was not something that was easily touched."

"You viewed her modest nature as being indifferent to Mr. Bingley," I determined, "and while there was a time that I would have disagreed with you, I have also begun to notice that she was making a grave mistake of showing less than what she felt rather than more."

"Did you advise her to do otherwise?"

"I persuaded her that she had nothing to lose by showing Mr. Bingley how much he meant to her."

"You were right to do so, for now that I see her heart in her eyes, I believe that she does care for him. Therefore, that impediment has been quite removed."

"And that was your real reason?"

"Yes, it was."

"Well, as much as I wish to find much fault with that view of the matter, I have to admit that you were quite right to be dubious of her intention. One cannot trust something that appears as non-existent. I knew her nature therefore I knew that she cared. Yet you did not know her true character, nor did Mr. Bingley, so exposing herself somewhat was a risk that she merely had to take."

"Thank you for advising her."

"Thank you for being willing to change your first impression of her. First impressions are hard things to overcome, I know."

"Yes, they are. Miss Elizabeth," Mr. Darcy continued, "while I am sure that you wish to return to Longbourn soon, in order to meet Mr. Collins, I just wish to inform you that Mr. Bingley does not feel imposed upon at all in you and your sister remaining. He enjoys the idea, as do I."

"I know he does, but you do as well?"

"Do you doubt me?"

"No, I do not. I just liked hearing your approval of us being here."

He gave me a steady glance. "You seek my approval?"

I leaned my head forward and chuckled. "Never, sir! Never, never, never!"

He laughed gently. "Oh, very well. Oh, and to confirm, since there shall be a ball here at Netherfield, I must ask a favor of you."

"Yes?"

"Actually, it is two favors."

"Ah, getting plural, are we?"

"Yes, my sister shall come to Netherfield Park soon and she is…my sister, Georgiana, is a lovely girl, but she is at the trying age, where her bashfulness gets the better of her. She and I are similar in that way. When she comes, can I rely upon you to help her be put at ease while she is here?"

"Oh, of course. I shall do my best, and to add to all this, I am sure that Jane would love to assist me."

"Yes, that would be very good of you both."

"And now, what is the second thing?"

"Oh, I shall be most content if you would do me the honor of securing your hand for the first two dances."

I put my hand to my chest. "Ah, that is the favor! Well, that is a favor that I am not afraid of. Though I do recall that there was a time when you did not think that I was handsome enough to tempt you."

"Oh, dear lord, I am never going to hear the end of that, am I?"

"Why, when it is always more fun to punish you for it? Funny. You have a sister, but you seem to have no idea of what the female consists of. A good memory is one of those things."

"I would even think to determine that you love to remember the things that one would wish you to forget, but then don't remember all the things we would wish for you to remember."

"That is a wonderfully wicked thing to determine."

He nodded, agreeing. "I am sure that it is."

"Well, I wonder now if I should retaliate and withdraw my offer to dance with you."

"You would do that?"

"Indeed, for as you know, the militia is now stationed here in Meryton, and I have only this day met an officer who would do this service with great credit."

"And who is this officer? Name the worthless miserable sot."

"Mr. Wickham."

When I said this, the mood changed so suddenly. Mr. Darcy, whose manner had been joking before, now looked on me coldly, his gaze stern and his brow creased with wrath.

"Mr. Darcy?"

"What did you say? His name was Mr. Wickham?"

"Yes."

"Mr. George Wickham?"

Surprised, I answered, "Yes. Do you know this man?"

Mr. Darcy stood up suddenly, walked over to the window and began to stare out of it, his hands fisted behind his back.

"Darcy, do you know this man?"

"Yes, I do. And we have a problem. Or I do, and it has followed me."

"Followed you?"

"Yes, and Miss Elizabeth, you must promise me this. Indeed, I will not stop until you promise me this."

"As long as you keep your promises to me, then I shall keep this one."

"Miss Elizabeth, please…"

"No, this is the way that it ought to be. I will not give you my word on things unless you treat me in the same style."

"Very well, I shall always keep my promises."

"Very good. Now I shall keep mine."

"Elizabeth, you must promise me to never trust him, never believe him, and if you can do so, never speak to him."

His words stunned me. "Never speak with him?"

"Yes, for I promise you this. He is the worst man in the world."

When Mr. Darcy told me this, my jaw dropped in surprise.

"Are you certain that we are speaking of the same Mr. Wickham?"

"Tall, almost my height, with curly brown hair, and lean but fit build, and a smooth voice."

Nodding, I answered, "Oh, yes, that is him. Yet what did you mean that he is the worst man in the world?"

Mr. Darcy closed his mouth and then looked back out of the window.

"Mr. Darcy, please, help me to understand. I cannot make a proper first impression based on prejudice that belonged to others who are not myself. If you want me to see this Mr. Wickham as you see him, then you must tell me the truth."

"Miss Elizabeth, I shall promise to tell you everything, but this secret does not belong to me, so you must promise to keep it."

I made an X over my heart. "I promise. I shall tell no one."

"Thank you. It is in regards to my sister, Georgiana. I must now mention a circumstance which I would wish to forget myself, and which no obligation less than the present should induce me to unfold to any human being.

"Having said thus much, I feel no doubt of your secrecy. My sister, who is more than ten years my junior, was left to the guardianship of my mother's nephew, Colonel Fitzwilliam, and me. About a year ago, she was taken from school, and an establishment formed for her in London. Last summer she went with the lady who presided over it to Ramsgate and thither also went Mr. Wickham, undoubtedly by design, for there proved to have been a prior acquaintance between him and Mrs. Younge, in whose character we were most unhappily deceived."

I watched as he clenched and unclenched his jaw.

"By her connivance and aid, he so far recommended himself to Georgiana. Her affectionate heart retained a strong impression of his kindness to her as a child, that she was persuaded to believe herself in love, and to consent to an elopement. She was then but fifteen, which must be her excuse, and after stating her imprudence, I am happy to add, that I owed the knowledge of it to herself.

"I joined them unexpectedly a day or two before the intended elopement, and then Georgiana, unable to support the idea of grieving and offending a brother whom she almost looked up to as a father, acknowledged the whole to me."

He turned from the window and glared at me. "You may imagine what I felt and how I acted. Regard for my sister's credit and feelings prevented any public exposure, but I wrote to Mr. Wickham, who left the place immediately, and Mrs. Younge was of course removed from her charge. Mr. Wickham's chief object was unquestionably my sister's fortune, which is thirty-thousand pounds, but I cannot help supposing that the hope of revenging himself on me was a strong inducement. His revenge would have been complete indeed. This, madam, is a faithful narrative of every event in which we have been concerned together."

When Mr. Darcy finished his tale, I covered my mouth.

"It is shocking indeed," I remarked, "for there is such an expression of goodness in his countenance and I never would have suspected it. All this time, he is the villain."

"Yes, and when my sister comes, if she is willing to tell you, she was violently in love with Mr. Wickham."

"He does have that effect. Oh, Miss Darcy must have been quite devastated."

"Yes, she could not have been more so."

"Then in reply, I am so very sorry for it. Then it must follow that we have to do everything in our power to keep Mr. Wickham from her presence."

"Yes. But there is something else through which I must ask you on. Should I inform her that he is present to begin with?"

"You have no choice," I offered. "For what if she comes upon him one day if we take her into town? She needs to know that he is here and that she ought not to be taken off guard."

"That is what alarms me. It shall hurt to tell her, but I have to try."

"Yes, you must. And she shall thank you for it. And when she is not at Netherfield, my sisters are very much willing to always be of assistance. Unless this Mr. Collins proves to be a distracting fellow."

"Pay no attention to him," Mr. Darcy stated firmly. "He is your younger sisters' problem, not yours."

"You seem determined to think ill of my cousin, Mr. Darcy," I noted, quite amused. "Be careful, for you are beginning to sound like my mother."

He threw his head back and laughed. "Oh, that very much has to be a first."

"Yes, it is. But Mr. Darcy, you spoke of how you were raised together at Pemberly."

He nodded, thoughtful. "Mr. Wickham was my father's steward's son, and my father quite doted on him. He paid for his university education, only for him to throw it away with his foolishness and worthlessness. When my father died, he was duped by Mr. Wickham's pleasing appearance and was as quick to believe as everyone else is. I swear, Mr. Wickham is a very fortunate man, for somehow, despite all of his horrible actions, people are always quick to believe in him."

"You sound as if you envied him."

"Yes, I suppose that I do. In one respect, I envy him very much."

I bit my lip, willing him to continue.

"You will not ask me the reason behind my envy. Well, perhaps you are wise. But I cannot be so. I must speak it."

I leaned toward him. "Then what is it? I am not wise myself, and indeed I am quite curious now."

"I envy that he is the sort of man who has the talent of conversing easily with people he has never met before. He has the talent of making a good first impression, and everyone is disposed to like him. Yes, he was born with all the appearance of goodness."

"While you were the one born with all the goodness, but not the appearance of it?" I guessed.

"Precisely. There you see, he is a fortunate man."

"Well, I understand that you cannot unveil your sister's secret unto the world but thank you for sharing with me this problem."

"You are most welcome. But Elizabeth, promise me to be careful, do not trust him, and if you speak to him, tell me afterwards, in case I need to intervene."

"Now who is the one being overprotective?"

"What can I say? I merely wished to return the compliment."

# Chapter Sixteen

## MR. COLLINS RUSHES IN

Of course, with Mr. Collins being now arrived at Longbourn, a letter was sent to us at Netherfield telling us of his presence there. Now fully renewed to health and strong enough, Jane and I were willing to walk to Longbourn from Netherfield, and Mr. Bingley would not hear tell of it. In fact, he wished to join us for our visit, but learned that he had some business to attend to, for he was invested in stock with Mr. Darcy. Therefore, Jane and I were willing to leave of our own accord, with the Bingley sisters at the stage where they never cared to accompany us anywhere, especially since they were quite against the idea of walking such a distance.

Mr. Bingley however had no real desire for us to walk back, for fear of Jane overtaxing herself, therefore, he promised to send his carriage for us by three o'clock in the afternoon.

When we disembarked, walking back home, Jane elaborated on her desire to walk with me rather than ride in a carriage.

"In truth," she explained, "I rather like the idea of being more self-sufficient now, and I have learned something."

"What?" I asked.

"Well, I love our mother and she means well, but sometimes her advice is not always so very sound. She always gave me instructions on how to be, and now I see that her lessons were all about how to shape my character in order to catch a husband. Yet perhaps it is better to have one's own way of being."

"You see now that there is nothing wrong with being a little… different. And outspoken."

Nodding, she answered, "Yes, I do enjoy it a great deal. Is this how it has always been with you, Lizzy? In your independent spirit?"

"Yes, it is. For better and for worse."

"Well, I suppose one cannot have a little better without having a bit of worse every now and again. But Lizzy, I must ask you."

"Yes?"

"What is your connection with Mr. Darcy precisely? I now know that it is not romantic, though I would wish it would be otherwise."

I looked at her, surprised. "Do you?"

"Yes, I do. For think on it, Liz. If Mr. Bingley were to choose me and Mr. Darcy were to choose you, then I feel as if nothing would ever separate us."

"Jane, I can think of nothing better, but while Mr. Darcy has been kind enough to flatter me and defend me against Miss Bingley's and Mrs. Hurst's criticisms, I do not believe that it is in the way of love."

"You don't?"

"No, but rather, I think that we are friends, in a strong way, or in a strange way. I just believe that we feel a bond, but it is not one designed by romantic notions."

"Are you certain of this, Lizzy?"

"I believe that I am not in error."

"It is just, I do not know if you are seeing the matter so very clearly and are not blinded in another quarter. You rushed to save his life, and he looks on you often, he depends on you. Is that not the very foundations of a true love?"

I wished that I could tell Jane how far I had come and how far I had gone into the world and all that I had seen, but one cannot do that. My adventure was my story and mine alone.

"Jane, I know that we were not taught otherwise, but I have learned, from all that I have seen, that there are more to relationships between men and women than just mother to son, brother to sister, father to daughter, and husband to wife. I have seen true friendship between men and women and that was all that there was between them. It is possible, we must believe, that it can be so."

"So, you have seen more than I? And what has taught you this?"

"I cannot name the moment or experience, but I feel that I have seen it somewhere." I grinned.

After two more miles of such a discussion, eventually we arrived at Longbourn.

When we reached the steps, the first person we met was Lydia, as she must have spied us from the window in her room.

"Lizzy and Jane, thank god you are come!" she groaned "For our cousin, Mr. Collins, has been here only one day and it can safely be said that he is the ghastliest man in England."

"Lydia, keep your voice down," Jane said. "And that is a harsh thing to say. It cannot be true."

"Oh, it is," Kitty confirmed, meeting us as we entered the vestibule. "You shall see, for it is not much to recommend there." She lowered her voice to a whisper. "Elizabeth and Jane, he is the worst sort of clergyman."

"And what is the wrong sort by your definition?" I asked.

"Whatever the wrong sort is, from this day forward, it shall always be called Mr. Collins."

And the wrong sort of clergyman Mr. Collins was indeed! When Jane and I announced ourselves, our mother burst in, with all eagerness.

"Ah, Jane and Lizzy! Our cousin, Mr. Collins is arrived from Kent; come and meet him."

Jane and I gave each other a look, then went into our sitting room to see our father sitting down in his favorite armchair. Near him stood Mary next to a tall and serious looking young man of his late twenties, and not one handsome feature to his countenance. That being said, while his looks were not much to recommend him, I worried that Kitty and Lydia were simply judging his character based solely on his looks. And if his disposition would prove to be lovely, then that would be unfair.

"Ah, so this must be the eldest sisters of the family," Mr. Collins began.

"Yes, they are indeed, sir," our mother replied. "This is my eldest, Jane, and the second of my children, Elizabeth."

"It is a pleasure to make your acquaintance, sir," Jane said curtsying, and I was left to curtsy behind her and note how Mr. Collins smiled at her first, and then I was an afterthought.

"My dear ladies." He bowed, his expression stern, and then he smiled suddenly at us. Yet this smile was strange, so inorganic, and to think in terms once more that were quite out of time, he seemed to be all time 'king of the trolls'.

It was clear that there was something quite off about his nature, but I did my best to refrain from another quick judgment. For some reason, I just did not wish to like him.

"Mr. Collins had proven to be punctual at his time," our mother said, wishing to build up his ego, I suppose. "For he came precisely at 4 o'clock the other day and shall stay for two whole weeks."

"Yes, it is a blessing that could not be foregone," our father added sarcastically, but Mr. Collins only grinned, missing the point and thinking my father gave him a compliment. "And indeed, the lord has smiled upon Longbourn with those two weeks."

"Oh, thank you, sir." Mr. Collins added. "And might I say the pleasure is all mine, for I have heard legends of your daughters' beauty and indeed, the rumors do not do them justice."

"Thank you, sir," I replied. "An acquaintance that begins with a compliment is always welcome."

"I was told that you were the witty one," he said, "and you must therefore be already doing it justice. While wit and humor are not always a welcome addition to young ladies, I suppose that I view it as being quite harmless and a very amusing thing."

I continued to smile, despite being offended. For something told me that Mr. Collins meant to pay a compliment but had no idea that he had insulted me. Yet I was meaning to do everything in my power to be careful, for if I showed him any offense at all, then I knew my fate, or our fate: he would marry Charlotte Lucas and Longbourn would be lost to us.

Our mother was correct in that way, that we did have to do everything in our power to be civil to him and make him feel affection for us. However, I knew my nature, and that was the sort to not hold someone who offended me for too long in my good graces. Therefore, I hoped that he did not keep up such comments, or over time, I would have no choice but to be myself and retaliate.

He sat down and began to speak with Jane and me, and we received him with politeness while Kitty and Lydia continually began to show signs of boredom.

"We don't mean to be disobliging," Kitty whispered to me when Mary was talking to Mr. Collins, "but it is just everything that he is saying are things that we heard yesterday, over and over again. And," she added, rolling her eyes, "wait till he gets onto the subject of his patron, Lady Catherine de Bourgh."

Unfortunately, Kitty had said the name a little too loudly, for Mr. Collins turned when we were speaking.

"Ah, Miss Kitty, did you mention my patroness's name there?"

"Oh, yes I did, sir," Kitty replied, not knowing what else to do, so I thought it wise to help her.

"She was just telling me about your good fortune on that score," I remarked, hoping I was close in the subject matter of what she was referencing. Luckily, I was, for Mr. Collins quickly smiled after that and began to shower me with much information on the famous lady.

Mr. Collins seemed neither in need of encouragement, nor inclined to be silent himself. He was very formal, which added to his heaviness somewhat, and Mary seemed to be enjoying being in his company.

Mary enjoyed his company! This very quickly got my mind thinking then, and if there was a chance that she would favor him, all would be well.

"Ah yes," Mr. Collins reported to Jane and me. "Miss Elizabeth, your curiosity does you much credit, for I have indeed been very fortunate to have been bestowed the position at Hunsford parsonage, where I believe that I shall have the talent of doing much good throughout the village. But as for my patroness, Lady Catherine de Bourgh's attention to my wishes, and consideration for my comfort, is very remarkable. And I do not believe that I could be more eloquent in praising her. For I have never in my life witnessed such behavior in a person of rank, such affability and condescension, as I have myself experienced from Lady Catherine.

"She has also asked me twice to dine at her estate, Rosings Park, imagine that! And she had sent for me only the Saturday before, to make up her pool of quadrille in the evening. She also has not the smallest objection to my joining in the society of the neighborhood or to my leaving the parish occasionally for a week or two, to visit my relations. She has even condescended to advise me to marry as soon as I could, provided I chose with discretion."

Here he turned and looked on Jane, who blushed and looked down at her hands on her lap.

"And she had once paid me a visit in my humble parsonage, where she had perfectly approved all the alterations I had been making and had even vouchsafed to suggest some herself: shelves in the closet upstairs."

"Shelves in the closest," I confirmed. "Well, now that is always a good thing."

"Yes, it is. A very good thing."

"Precisely," Mary added. "She seems to be a very attentive neighbor, and that is always well. It has often been said, sir, that good advice is like good wine; it gets better with age."

"Yes, well…" Mr. Collins trailed off, and I could tell that he had no idea what to say.

"Does she live near you, sir?" Mary also asked, "Lady Catherine de Bourgh, I mean."

"The garden in which stands my humble abode is separated only by a lane from Rosings Park, her ladyship's residence."

"I think you said she was a widow, sir?" Jane asked, "Has she any family?"

"She has only one daughter, the heiress of Rosings, and of very extensive property."

"Ah! Then she is better off than many girls," our mother retorted. "And what sort of young lady is she? Is she handsome?"

Mr. Collins then began to praise Miss de Bourgh, and it left me to believe that his favoring his post might have led to him having a blind eye toward any flaws in his patroness and her daughter. Yet until I met the women behind his praises, I would be none the wiser.

As we sat down to our meal, Mr. Collins looked at us all again, and I felt as if he was appraising us in some way. Yet, he actually was in fact doing so, and his continual looks at Jane confirmed my suspicions. Yet even if not so, the answer to his intention for coming was proved in the next moment.

"I still cannot help but reiterate," he continued, "that I had heard much of their beauty, but that in this instance fame had fallen short of the truth. And I do not doubt, Mrs. Bennet, that very soon you shall see them all in due time disposed of in marriage."

"You are very kind," our mother replied. "I am sure, and I wish with all my heart it may prove so, for else they will be destitute enough. Things are settled so oddly."

He nodded sagely. "You allude, perhaps, to the entail of this estate."

"Ah! Sir, I do indeed. It is a grievous affair to my poor girls, you must confess. Not that I mean to find fault with *you*, for such things I know are all chance in this world. There is no knowing how estates will go when once they come to be entailed."

"I am very sensible, madam, of the hardship to my fair cousins, and could say much on the subject, but that I am cautious of appearing forward and precipitate. But I can assure the young ladies that I come prepared to admire them. At present I will not say more but, perhaps, when we are better acquainted—"

Then he stopped and looked at Jane again.

And it was most clear.

Mr. Collins had come to find himself a wife.

Of course this realization was kind in one way, for to consider us first for a wife was very courteous of him. Yet Mr. Collins's pleasing attentions toward Jane did not bode well, so when there was a moment of time alone with my mother, I had to caution her.

"Mama, Mr. Collins looks at Jane a great deal."

"Yes, he does, I have noticed," she replied.

"But while Mr. Bingley has not made her an official offer, is it not best, that when there is a moment to inform him, tell Mr. Collins of her being potentially soon engaged? I just think Mr. Bingley needs a little time."

"Oh Lizzy, never fear, I am very much prepared on that score. The second he shows any real interest, I shall inform him of the matter at once, and that you four are the only options open to him. After all, one of you should be able to do for his tastes."

"But, Mama, you may not...that is to say... Mama, surely you are not considering me for him?"

"Lizzy, of course I am. You are not to be exempt from your sisters in this matter."

My discomfort grew. "But Mama, I do not like him."

"You have only just met him, therefore, how do you know if you like him or not?"

"Mother, please do not encourage him on this matter for me. Mary likes him only. Encourage him to pursue that."

"Mary likes him?"

Our mother turned to Mary and saw that in fact Mary was speaking with him with alacrity and eagerness. She was attentive, and of course she was, for to marry a clergyman was something that suited her tastes more than anyone of us left.

"Yes, she does. And you know Lydia. She is not meant to be a clergyman's wife, and Kitty is similar. And as for myself," I began, taking my mother's shoulder and looking imploringly into her eyes. "Mama, please. I love you, I do. And I wish to make you happy, but now please still see me for who I am. You know my nature, and I am not meant for his sort either. Please protect me now, and let me be as I am. I am not made for Mr. Collins. You know it."

When I said this, with much supplication, my mother was affected, and she faltered.

"What has changed with us, Lizzy?" she asked gently. "For you have been so much more open to me than of late."

"Well, I suppose that I realized that I do not have all the time in the world. Mama, please, really how much do I ask for?"

"But if he takes a fancy to you, Lizzy, what could I say to deter him and shift his gaze toward Mary?"

"Well, he clearly shall have to shift his gaze from Jane soon, therefore can you not encourage Mary's suit, and Mary's alone?"

My mother looked away from me and at Mr. Collins again.

"Well, Lizzy, if this is what your heart wants, then yes I shall attempt to do it."

"Thank you, Mama." I kissed her cheek, then rubbed her shoulder and walked away.

෨෪෨

"I have made the most wonderful discovery," Mr. Collins said, after he had spoken to Jane. "I was told that you are staying at Netherfield Park, which belongs to a man named Bingley, but Miss Bennet here has just told me that one of his main guests is a gentleman named Mr. Fitzwilliam Darcy."

"Yes, that is correct," I acknowledged.

"Mr. Fitzwilliam Darcy of Pemberly?"

"Yes. Are you acquainted with him?"

"No, but I must make myself acquainted with him at once, for he is the nephew of my esteemed patroness, Lady Catherine."

"Lady Catherine de Bourgh is Mr. Darcy's aunt?"

"Yes, she is. And to discover that you are living in the same home as him at present. Well, I feel now as if providence itself has sent me here, and my favoring my family with a visit now has raised this time in Hertfordshire higher in my eyes."

Ah, he would raise his esteem for us merely by the association we had with another household. Yes, his character was now quite fixed and clear to me. Mr. Collins was not a sensible man, and the deficiency of nature had been, but little assisted by education or society, that much was clear.

A fortunate chance had recommended him to Lady Catherine de Bourgh when the living of Hunsford was vacant, I was left to conclude, and the respect which he felt for her high rank, and his veneration for her as his patroness, mingling with a very good opinion of himself, of his authority as a clergyman, and his right as a rector, made him altogether a mixture of pride and obsequiousness, self-importance and humility.

All it took was a proud remark here, a foolish acknowledgment there, and every now and again a ridiculous thought offered by him in between, for this all to be quite determined.

"He tried to read Fordyce's Sermons to us last night," Lydia said to me. "That I was driven quite to distraction, could not sit still, and had to interrupt him because I could not bear it any longer."

"And you were even more wild than usual," Mary told her as she passed us. "For here our guest was, in hopes of enlightening your mind and you handed it over as a moment to ridicule."

"You like conduct books, Mary, because you are one."

"I have to be, for it counteracts your lack of ability to be one."

"I would not touch a conduct book if my life depended on it!"

"Fortunately for you, it never shall."

"Oh, the two of you, really," I said, having enough of them as I excused myself to go to my room and have a moment alone. Once I got there, I opened my door and realized that I had not been in my bedroom for so very long!

And yet, there it was all the same. I walked in, closed the door behind me and twirled around. Nothing shall ever make up for how it feels to be home, and I lay on my bed, quite content. Staring up at the ceiling, I wished that life would never change now. Having released any hope of seeing Mr. Darcy again in the future, and hoping that he would move on as long as he did not go back to Caroline after what she had done, I was now resigned to it all, and was instead hoping that life would remain static.

I never wanted us to lose Longbourn, and wished for us to remain there always, except for Jane, who would one day live at Netherfield Park as mistress. Yet this room, no in fact, I never wished to lose it at all, even to my dear friend Charlotte.

Yet all things eventually come to an end, therefore I soon had to return downstairs where the carriage would arrive to return us to Netherfield.

I knew that my sisters were in the backyard, playing a game of horseshoes. As I went down the steps, I heard hushed voices. Quieting my footsteps, I neared the drawing room, and in fact it was the voices of my mother and Mr. Collins.

"Mrs. Bennet," he began, "as you might have already surmised, I have been bestowed a parsonage of no mean size."

"Yes, and I even have remembered the name: Hunsford!"

"Thank you. Having now a good house and a very sufficient income, I do not deny that I greatly desire a mistress for it. For as you know, my patroness, the noble and honorable Lady Catherine de Bourgh, had specifically recommended it. In fact, she has decreed it: 'Mr. Collins,' she always said, 'you must marry!'

"And since her advice is always vital to me, mingled with the fact that all clergymen ought to set a good example of matrimony in their parish, and as you know, I have a great parish indeed, also seeking reconciliation with the Longbourn family, who as you know I hold you all in great reverence and respect…"

My god, when was he going to get to the point? He kept speaking this way, over and over and all I could do was wait and risk much by eavesdropping. Yet finally, after a few more sentences spoken, mingled with compliments and apologies, he finally got to the point.

"I admit now," he concluded, "that with my living and station in life, as well as wishing to eliminate any ill-will done to your family by this entail, I came to Longbourn specifically in want of a wife. And here at Longbourn, seeing your set of radiant daughters, I feel confident that I am worthy of the attentions of one of them, as well as them being worthy of me.

"This is my plan of amends—of atonement—for inheriting their father's estate. And I flatter myself, that I found that to be quite an excellent idea, full of eligibility and suitableness, and excessively generous and disinterested on my own part."

"Yes, it is indeed," our mother said. "And you do us great honor so…"

"Therefore, I am quite struck by your daughters' charms. Especially the eldest Miss Bennet."

"Oh, thank you, yes Jane is admired wherever she goes, but Mr. Collins I must warn you that she shall soon be engaged to another gentleman."

"Oh, that is most unfortunate."

"But as to my *younger* daughters, I could not take upon me to say—I could not positively answer—but I did not *know* of any prepossession."

"Oh, so they are available."

"Yes, sir. Is there any other in the set that you can turn your mind to? For I can assure you that they all are sweet girls, though I say it myself."

He appeared slightly befuddled. "Well, the eldest not being available does shift my gaze and set me back. Yet I am one to always prefer and favor the eldest, for it is, I always feel, proper to respect rank in such a way. Therefore, I feel that it is most proper therefore to shift my attentions quite easily to your second oldest, Miss Elizabeth. After all, I give respect to her age, and she is also the nearest to her older sister in beauty as well."

"Oh, thank you, Mr. Collins; that is a marvelous idea."

When hearing this, my heart turned cold. My mother had promised me so very faithfully, and I thought she would stand by my side in my preferences, but she would not. I felt so forlorn and slightly betrayed. Did my happiness mean nothing to her? And now she was encouraging Mr. Collins to marry me!

Yet as I stood there, I heard my mother shift, and then she continued to speak.

"However," she continued, "I have been very fortunate, for I do not have one daughter being sought after, but a second. While Jane shall very soon be engaged, Lizzy is in the midst of the beginnings of a courtship as well, and therefore she is unable to be pursued in any other quarter. I am honored by your intentions, sir, but my two eldest daughters are quite out of the question."

I breathed a sigh of relief. My mother had not abandoned me and therefore she had done her best to help me with what I wished to do. I was rash to have gotten angry as quickly as I had, because she had in fact only been building up to her promise, and I was safe.

"Now," she continued, "as to the youngest, Mr. Collins of *them* I know nothing at all about any prior attachment. Yet if I may be so bold and since you are choosing based also on the oldest age, might I recommend you shifting your attentions toward my third daughter, Mary? She is a dear sweet girl, attends to her studies, respects your choice of books, and has always enjoyed doing work for the church."

"Miss Mary?"

"Yes, sir, I can assure you, that she is the perfect choice for you, sir, and shall make you a splendid wife."

"Miss Mary…well, I believe that *that* perhaps would be an excellent suggestion!"

I closed my eyes in relief. Mr. Collins was now set on the right course.

# Chapter Seventeen

## MR. DARCY'S SISTER

Before I left Longbourn, I hugged my mother tenderly, happy that she had listened to me so very well and was willing to help me and let me choose my path. In that moment, I realized that our relationship very much had changed. I believe that she was seeing me differently than she had before, and she was accepting me at last.

When we returned to Netherfield Park, Mr. Bingley was once more attentive toward Jane, and by his side, was Mr. Darcy.

"How was your time back home?" he asked when he accosted me.

"It was as it always is when one returns home," I replied, removing my bonnet. "It was indescribably comfortable. I suppose that is how you feel when you are back at Pemberly."

He smiled at me. "Oh, that is precisely how I am."

I grinned in return. "You are smiling. That is very good, and I am happy for it."

"So am I. So, how was your meeting with your cousin, Mr. Collins?"

"I believe that things may potentially work out to everyone's satisfaction, and he has taken a fancy to my younger sister, Mary."

"That is very good then?"

"Yes, it is, Mr. Darcy, and it makes me feel quite happy. For out of the five of us, he shall choose the one that is most taken with him."

"Then that is good, and you have no reason to worry?"

"No, there is not. I look very happy, don't I?"

"Yes, you do."

"It's because I am. So, when are we to have the pleasure of your sister's company here at Netherfield?"

"If all goes according to plan, she shall arrive here in two days' time, in the mid-afternoon."

And in two days' time, at mid-afternoon, we were all gathered outside of Netherfield Park, as a carriage pulled up and was parked before us. The door opened, Mr. Darcy went to it, gave the young woman inside his hand, and finally she emerged into the light. That was our first sight of Miss Georgiana Darcy.

"My dear Georgiana!" Caroline Bingley declared, coming forward and taking Georgiana's hand. "My dear, you are truly in the best of looks and we welcome you to Netherfield Park."

"Thank you, Miss Bingley," Georgiana said in a quiet voice. "It is a pleasure to see you again as well."

"We have been quite forlorn without you," Mrs. Hurst said, then she turned to Mr. Hurst. "Haven't we, Mr. Hurst?"

Mr. Hurst had not been paying attention at the time, so he turned when hearing his name and did not know what she was talking about.

"What?"

Mrs. Hurst rolled her eyes, looked away from her husband and back at Georgiana, who then turned to us.

"Georgiana," Mr. Darcy said, "allow me to introduce to you two guests here. This is Miss Jane Bennet and Miss Elizabeth Bennet of Longbourn."

"Miss Darcy," Jane said, "welcome to Hertfordshire."

I smiled at her warmly. "Yes, you are most welcome."

"Thank...thank you," she replied, and then she turned to me. "My brother has told me so much about you that I feel as if I know you both already. And you, you were the angel who saved my brother."

"I had the help of a studious stable hand, but yes, I did."

"In fact, Miss Darcy," Caroline added, "it really was Mr. Watson, our employee, who had carried Mr. Darcy in."

"And it was Miss Elizabeth who had given me the very air from her lungs to save mine," Mr. Darcy continued, avoiding Caroline's eyes. Realizing that she had been quite hushed up, she smiled forcefully, took Georgiana's arm and led her into the house.

"Come," she and Mrs. Hurst said. "We have so much to get you acquainted with."

At first when Georgiana arrived, there was no chance of Jane and I getting to speak with her, for Caroline and Mrs. Hurst quite dominated her, asking about every detail of her life since last they saw her.

Initially, Mr. Darcy just sat there and watched, and then he came and sat down beside me.

"I suppose that I am quite failing to make your sister feel at home," I observed.

He leaned toward me. "Because you are not being given the opportunity."

"I do believe the sisters do not wish for me to get a word in edgewise."

"I'd say that I don't know why they are your enemies, but I know why they are."

"Could you tell me then? For I am quite at a loss. Besides being a slight imposition, I do them no harm. Well, besides the few times that I steal attention from Miss Bingley, I am guiltless. She perhaps just only wishes for your attention and because I get in the way of it, she cannot forgive me? Is that correct?"

He raked his fingers through his thick hair. "Ah, I was wondering when we were ever going to speak about that."

"Yes, well, now is as good a time as any. I wish that I could tell her that she has nothing to fear from me, and from your admiring my 'fine eyes', but I do not believe that she would listen."

"No, no she would not."

"Therefore, I shall have to be content with always being the most hated person in the room. Yet you do not despise me, and therefore that is of great comfort."

"I am happy that it is. Now if you shall excuse me, I have to find a way to get my sister away from Miss Bingley's fierce gaze and I can only think of it in one way."

"What way is that?"

"I must sacrifice myself."

"Sacrifice yourself? How so?"

"For the moment, I must give Miss Bingley myself."

I laughed softly as Mr. Darcy stood up and asked Caroline if she would take a turn about the room with him, for it was most refreshing. Caroline was overjoyed by this, stood up, took his arm and began to walk about the room, and then, before she could feel herself so favored and flattered by this, Mr. Darcy asked Mrs. Hurst if she also would join them.

Having no choice but to agree, Mrs. Hurst took his other arm, they walked around the room together, and that left Georgiana quite alone.

Thus, I stood up, walked over to her, and took the place of where the Bingley Hydras had just been.

"So, we get to speak at last," I began as I sat down.

"Yes, we do," Georgiana said, and her voice was soft and a little uncertain. "Miss Elizabeth, I cannot thank you enough for the service that you had rendered my brother in saving his life. I owe you everything."

"You feel as if you owe me everything, when you really owe me nothing. It was my pleasure, and I would do it again for him in a heartbeat. Yet I am glad that when you learned of it, you were intent to come and be with him. Such sisterly affection always has to be admired."

"You would know about that as well," Georgiana said. "Fitzwilliam told me in a letter about how you walked three miles so that you could look after your sister, Jane, when she was sick here."

"Yes, indeed I did. So, we both have had the fate of traveling far and wide for our siblings in their time of need."

She gave me a lovely smile. "Yes, yes we have. But I suppose that I am lucky that your sister fell ill, because if she had not, then you would not have come, and if you would not have come, then you would not have been able to save a life that was so very important to me."

"You love him a great deal, don't you?"

"Yes, I do. He is the best older brother that there could be."

"Is he indeed?"

"Yes, I could not wish for a better one."

"You make him sound ideal, and therefore I am quite jealous of you now. I have no brothers, only four sisters."

"Oh, that must be delightful. I have always wanted a sister."

"And I have always wanted a brother. We both were left wanting something, but I suppose that is just the way of life, isn't it? To always want something."

"Yes, I suppose that it is. It is quite vexing, isn't it?"

"Yes, it is. But Miss Darcy, I actually have a secret to tell you."

"A secret?"

"Yes, and you shall perhaps think my family is shameless after this, but I believe you to be the understanding sort; we are not perfect."

"Whatever do you mean?" she asked, lowering her voice in a very conspiratorial way. I believed that my scheme was working.

"In truth, when Jane had to stay the night here for the first time, it was not an accident."

"I was told that she took a horse here for a tete e tete with the sisters, but when she was caught in the rain, she had to stay the night and then she fell ill."

"The falling ill was an accident, but the reason why Jane rode a horse rather than take a carriage was because my mother believed that it would rain and if it did, then Jane would have to stay the night, and therefore, it would give her a chance to stay here."

"Why did your mother want Jane to stay?"

"Promise that you shall not tell a soul of this."

Her eyes were wide. "I promise."

"Well, my sister is smitten on Mr. Bingley."

Georgiana looked at my sister, who was speaking to Mr. Bingley and she saw how close they were to each other, and she realized what I was implying. When she realized it, she gasped, smiling. "Your mother did that?"

"Yes, she did. In hopes that it would give them a chance to fall in love, my mother used her superior telling of the weather to orchestrate affection.

"At first Jane and I did not like this, especially after she fell ill, but then what would have happened if she didn't? If she wasn't what she was? Jane never would have gotten sick, I never would have come, and I never would have found your brother. So, I suppose, that this whole day came about because my mother is...my mother."

"Amazing, is it not? That one decision could have changed the course of so many things."

"Yes, yes, it is."

We both looked up as Mr. Darcy passed us by with the Bingley sisters. As he did so, he winked at us both, and Georgiana and I turned toward each other and giggled.

Whatever were Georgiana's faults, the worst of them was simply being shy, and since that was the case, she proved to be a delightful woman and had much to recommend her. Mostly we sat with the Bingley sisters, who dominated her, but their behavior was so forced that I knew very well that Georgiana was never fully at ease.

Georgiana's nature, so modest, artless, easy in manner, and just a little self-conscious, also mixed well with Jane's serene nature and they also got along splendidly.

Yet as time between the ball drew on, Jane and I finally had to accept that it was time for us to return home. Therefore, at last we returned to Longbourn, and Mr. Collins still was in residence there. Of course, he very much wished to become acquainted with Mr. Darcy and his sister, for he did not get the chance to visit Netherfield in our time.

This was easy to agree to, because Georgiana promised us a visit with her brother, and this worried me greatly. After all, Mr. Collins, over time, had proved to be even more ridiculous than I could imagine, and then perhaps Lydia and Kitty's nature could be a little trying to Georgiana's natural simplicity.

However, when the Netherfield party did visit us at Longbourn, I had the good fortune to have no need to worry. All came to visit; my mother was beside herself, for they were staying for a mid-day meal, and while the Bingley sisters naturally did not care to speak to her, my younger sisters, or me, Georgiana surprised us all, because she actually took to Lydia and Kitty quite well.

Say what you will of them both, but their manners were artless, and their rambunctious ways can put someone at ease due to their natures being so open. Lydia was vulgar and crass, but she was no liar. Kitty was a bit of a follower and could be easily manipulated, but she was true, harmless and happy to make a friend. Therefore, I suppose it was only natural that Georgiana and Kitty especially would get along. Kitty just wished to get along well with whoever she met, and since Georgiana was lovely, kind and exotic to her, Kitty was quite on her best behavior. Whatever vulgarity that Lydia had, it was perhaps just amusing to Georgiana, who as she had told me, always wanted a sister of her own. Perhaps our set of sisters at Longbourn was the sort of company that she always had wanted. We weren't perfect but we were real.

Yet Mr. Collins was another matter. Once he was acquainted with Mr. Darcy and Miss Darcy, there was no saving that situation. He would compliment them, often tell Mr. Darcy about Lady Catherine's good health and about all that Lady Catherine had told him in regards to his daily activities.

By the time that Mr. Darcy and his company were meant to leave, I am sure that he had learned of what Lady Catherine first wore when she had him ordained at Hunsford, what her first words to Mr. Collins were, when she first visited him at the parsonage, what were her notes on his first sermon, what she liked most to eat, what was her advice to one of the parishioners who could not decide what governess was best for her children, and who was the best apothecary in the county of that part of Kent.

When I finally got a moment to speak to him, I could tell that he was most put out by the end of it and I knew that he wanted nothing more than to quit Longbourn immediately.

"Mr. Darcy," I said, as I joined him as he stared out of our window, a clear sign of retreat. "I trust that we have become close enough friends that you will not hold one horrible relation against us."

"Miss Elizabeth, he told me about how many shelves my aunt recommended that he should put into one of his closets."

I shook my head. "I have no doubt about that, and while such folly in others usually amuses me, this time, I regret that you have to see it. But please, Mr. Darcy, we have come so far. Do not forsake us now for this one bad impression."

"You think I shall eliminate my good opinion of you because of one cousin?" he asked me most directly.

"Well, you almost did it to Jane once before. Surely you cannot blame me for worrying now."

"Oh, I suppose you are correct."

"I just want to make sure that you shall not turn away from us. We can't be held responsible for others."

His smile was warm. "I suppose so, though if he begins to tell me about curtains she may have recommended, I shall have to quit the house."

I bit my lip to keep from smiling. "You would be frightened by such a subject."

"Ah, do not mock me."

I couldn't help but laugh. "I mock you very much, for mocking you always puts you at ease."

"Oh, very well, it might. My sister has taken quite well to you, Miss Elizabeth, as I very well knew that she would."

"I am happy for it. She is a sweet and steady girl. And she loves you very much."

"As I do love her. In truth, I wasn't always the best older brother."

"No need to worry. Being a sibling is like many things in this world; it takes practice. Besides, it's not always about how you start, but how you get there in the end. And you both have clearly gotten to that point in your lives where all is well."

He nodded, agreeing. "Yes, yes, we have. How far we have come, and yet still there is more to go."

"There always is."

He turned to me. "And I must confess, that I had no idea that she would take to your younger sisters so well. But she has."

"They are of the same age. Therefore, they are likeminded in that way, I suppose. And whatever my sisters' faults, they are pleasant girls who can make good company for those who prefer their tempers and personalities."

"I believe my sister was simply lonely."

"That is normal."

"And there are things which I cannot ever do for her. The simple acts of women being closely bound to each other. I confess when Bingley and I first became friends, I was hoping she and Miss Bingley would become close friends, but their natures were so different and…"

I slanted him a look. "And what?"

"Do not repeat this, Miss Elizabeth."

"You know that I won't, so tell all."

"Well, in truth, Miss Bingley actually quite scared Georgiana."

I tried not to laugh but didn't succeed. "That I can easily believe."

"You ought to," He laughed with me.

Our attention was caught however when Mr. Collins passed us, and he was speaking to Mary.

"Sixty-four windows," he was saying. "Her Ladyship has sixty-four windows in total and the blazing alone cost…"

"Oh, my god," Mr. Darcy hissed silently to me, "now he is talking about my aunt's windows. Why is the blasted man talking about her windows?"

"Who knows?" I suppressed a smile. "Maybe he likes windows."

"He likes money."

"Everyone likes money," I agreed.

"Yes, but he's like a weasel with it."

"Yes, he is. But promise me that you shall not lose respect for us because of it."

"I promise, I shall not."

"Thank you, Mr. Darcy. That is of great comfort."

We looked at each other, smiled and then looked out of the window.

"We do this a lot, don't we?" I asked. "Look out of windows."

"Yes, well it's more like I do it and you have no choice but to join me. So, tell me now, I see that Mr. Collins is paying much attention to your younger sister, Mary."

"Yes, he is."

"Then there is hope there. If so, then you shall not lose Longbourn."

"Yes, we shall not."

"I am happy for you, because you deserve it."

"Thank you."

"Fitzwilliam and Miss Elizabeth," Georgiana said, getting pulled along by Kitty, "we are going outside to play horseshoes."

"Very well," Mr. Darcy said, and the three of them exited, went to the lawn where we saw my sisters and his play from the window.

"I never thought to ever see Mr. Darcy's little sister here at Longbourn," I remarked, "and to see her playing with sisters of mine."

"I never would have thought it either, but here we are. And I quite like it."

"So do I."

# Chapter Eighteen

## THE IMBECILE

The next day, our party of Longbourn walked into town with Charlotte and Maria Lucas. While the future had shown me that Charlotte and Mr. Collins had gotten married, the present was proving that to not be a very fixed thing.

Mr. Collins smiled and was kind to the Lucas sisters, but his attention was focused solely on Mary, as it ought to have been. They were both similar in mind, intention and motives, therefore I wondered, in looking at them happily together, why in the alternate reality had he chosen to marry Charlotte when Mary was always right there? Why would he have not chosen Mary from the very beginning? What could have changed between then and now?

And then the answer came to me.

There was only one difference.

Me.

In that initial reality of how our lives played out, I was the only subject of variance. In some way, I had done something to change the flow of our paths, and while I very well may have never discovered what that difference was, I could only tell my own actions in a step by step process:

Jane had fallen in love with Mr. Bingley.

I went to look after her.

In the process, I had saved Mr. Darcy's life.

This action left Mr. Bingley and Darcy to feel indebted to my family, so Mr. Bingley allowed Jane to remain.

Now Jane was no longer available.

That was it!

Jane was no longer available for Mr. Collins to choose and be rejected by. After all, while Jane would do anything to help our family and be obliging, I knew her nature, and she could never find herself to be the sort to marry without falling in love. Jane could and would never marry Mr. Collins…therefore there was only one thing to determine.

In the first reality, Jane must've rejected Mr. Collins! Yes, of course, that had to have been the cause of it all. I still would be shocked by her doing so, but that must've been what happened. He offered a marriage proposal to her, and she refused him, making him turn to another woman, and that was Charlotte, out of spite. That had to have been it. After all, what other possibility could it have been?

Either way, it was clear now more than ever that time could be re-written. But in the future, if time could be undone, would the other Mr. Darcy know the difference? Would he have two memories in his mind: the one where Mr. Collins married Charlotte Lucas, or the one where his ancestor survived and so Mr. Collins married my sister Mary?

I hoped that my actions were not the sort to cause havoc to the natural order of things. I hoped that I had not saved a life in the present and therefore altered the course of the future in a negative way in later years, but I could not think about that at present.

All that I could see at the moment was how Mary and Mr. Collins walked side by side, most animated as they spoke and enjoying being likeminded individuals. And Charlotte was walking alongside me and Maria, and was nowhere near Mr. Collins, as if their futures would never be intertwined.

And yet, my heart did secretly reach out to Charlotte, whose life had changed in a desire to put my own life into order. Therefore, in some ways, I had hurt her. However, when she had chosen to marry Mr. Collins, she would have had no scruples on hurting my family, therefore it was simply us all doing the best we could with the hand that fate had dealt us.

Yet Charlotte, as she walked beside me, was happy and carefree, enjoying our conversation. Therefore, all my worrying was pointless, because this was all unknown to her. She missed nothing, and therefore perhaps I had saved her as well: she was too wise for a man like Mr. Collins. Now she could save herself for a better man or face the reality that it was better to be single rather than married to the most ridiculous man in all of England.

We entered Meryton and soon we came upon a company of officers. Among them were Denny, Captain Carter, Colonel Forster and his wife, Mrs. Forster, who was very great friends with Lydia especially. Yet also among them, tall as a tree it seemed, was Mr. Wickham, now dressed in his regimental uniform.

We immediately joined their company after introducing Mr. Collins to them. As our companies mixed and mingled with each other, Mr. Wickham, for some reason, liked the idea of approaching me.

"How do you do this day, Miss Elizabeth?"

"I am very well, thank you, Mr. Wickham. And now you are here, in your regimentals."

"Yes, and he shall out-class us all, eh, Wickham?" Denny said.

"Denny, you exaggerate, I am sure," Mr. Wickham said. "I neither swagger nor strut."

"Wait a few years, and then you shall."

"Well now, Miss Elizabeth, how are you this day?" he asked again.

"I am well, Mr. Wickham. We at Longbourn are all well, thank you."

"You are most welcome."

"Are you excited for the Netherfield Ball? For when I last heard, you officers were also invited as well."

"Yes, and the invitation has spread joy in more than one quarter."

"Therefore, you wish to come and shall?"

"No, by no means unfortunately am I able. In truth, business calls me away to town, for in fact, there is a gentleman among Mr. Bingley's company who I wished greatly to avoid."

"Truly?" I asked innocently. "Who would it be?"

"Miss Elizabeth, can I confide in you?"

"You may."

"This is a great secret, and I speak it with you, because you appear to be of a trusting nature."

"I thank you for the compliment. I shall listen with all sincerity."

"The man is... Mr. Darcy. I have no reason to avoid him except that he has done me a great wrong."

Ah, the other side to the story. "How did he wrong you?"

"He and I were raised together actually at Pemberly. Yes, Miss Elizabeth, we grew up together, but his father loved me so much that he left me the living of Kempton where I would run the church there, as vicar. Yet when Mr. Darcy senior had passed away, his son refused, point blank, to offer me the estate that his father left me. So, you see, I have been forced to make my way in the world, all at the hands of Mr. Darcy."

"How could he have not given you an estate that was left to you in his father's will?" I asked, again innocently.

"Oh, it was very complicated, for in the will, the living was left to me in a conditional way, and it was hard to argue it."

"And you took no legal action?"

"It was too hard of a thing to argue."

"Really? Well, I am sorry that you were so imposed upon, but just to inform you, for you seem to be misinformed. But Mr. Darcy is not only in residence at Netherfield Park, but so is his sister, Miss Darcy. I am sure that you are well acquainted with her, for you were raised at Pemberly."

When I mentioned Georgiana, Mr. Wickham's face altered, and he appeared much discomforted.

"Yes, I am well acquainted with her. When I was a child, she and I were good friends, and I devoted hours and hours to her amusement. She also went through a stage when she reached her older years where her attitude toward me changed, and I never see her now. How was she when you met her?"

"She is one of the loveliest women that I have ever met, and I liked her very much. Indeed, I find nothing wanting in her character."

"Yes, well I am very glad that you liked her, for I have been told that she has improved uncommonly well of late and that she is now as good a woman as any."

"Perhaps it is because she is no longer troubled by the attentions of a pernicious suitor."

When I said this, all the color from Mr. Wickham's face drained and he turned quite pale with slight alarm.

"And perhaps," I continued, "it is because she is no longer dogged by a man who professes to be in love with her, when she is but a child and he was a grown man. Then when it was made clear that he was merely marrying her for her wealth and he would not receive any of her dowry if he married her, he quitted Pemberly immediately and left Miss Darcy quite devastated by all the lies that he offered her. Yes, that would be enough to make any woman a far better creature, for she was removed from the wrong sort of man. Would you not agree, Mr. Wickham?"

Mr. Wickham did not reply, but only nodded his head slightly.

"Mr. Wickham, I shall say this once. This story that you tell, it is lies.

Do not spread them, for if there is one thing that can combat a lie, it is the truth. It is always the truth. And you will have brought a hard fate on yourself. Therefore, reform and improve yourself, sir, and the life you save may be your own."

Mr. Wickham did not look at me as he nodded to me once more and then left me to talk with Lydia.

And thus, I was released from one of the most deceitful men in England.

All throughout our walk with the officers, I pretended to be aloof but I observed Mr. Wickham for the whole of it, and he never left Lydia's side, for with her, he had an audience that would never tire of his attentions. Yet I knew very well that I had nothing to worry about with letting her talk to him. For he was an imbecile, but a mercenary one, and Lydia had no money, therefore she was not in any sort of danger.

# Chapter Nineteen

## THE BALL TO END ALL BALLS

The days leading up to Netherfield Ball had gone by speedily enough, and we residents of Longbourn found ourselves in a long line of carriages to enter the house.

"And to think Lizzy," Jane whispered to me as our carriage was being parked, "that we lived here for almost a month complete, and now we are returning to it."

"I think your Mr. Bingley missed you being there."

"Oh, but Lizzy, he is not my Mr. Bingley."

"Not yet, but any day that idea may change."

Eventually we entered the house and met the family. As we went through the crowd, I spotted Mr. Darcy and Georgiana, and we Bennets immediately rushed to them. To see us able to converse with them so easily was quite marvelous, for indeed we really had grown to be affectionate toward each other. But it really was the presence of Georgiana, for her desire for our company allowed Mr. Darcy the comfort to open up and accept us, despite any societal differences that may have impeded our unification before.

He even was able to overlook Mr. Collins's foolishness rather than care for it at all. But Jane and I did our best to make sure that Mary kept Mr. Collins's attention throughout the evening. However, it could be said, that in a prudential light, he distracted her as well, because when the time of the evening came for some musical entertainment, she was so absorbed by his narration about what his duties were to his parish and to Lady Catherine, that she didn't even care to get up and show off her skill at the pianoforte, but rather only sat and spoke with him.

I made sure to often remain close to Charlotte as well, and I looked on her as Mary was often seen beside Mr. Collins and sought to mark any looks of envy. But there were none. In fact, Charlotte was quite pleased at the idea.

"Well, Mary does seem very well pleased with Mr. Collins."

"Yes. Yes, she is. I am quite happy for her, for Mary is the one out of us five who I am convinced has any chance of living happily with him."

"Yes, she would, and I am not surprised. Also, she is wise, for unlike Jane at first, Mary has appeared to do all in her power to show him her heart and look what has become of it. She indeed has helped him on, and therefore, I am most convinced that in no more than a couple of months, Mr. Collins shall make her an offer."

"An offer that she cannot refuse," I said before I could catch myself. As I said it, I almost bit my lip, for I could not believe that I had let such a 20th century cinematic phrase slip into my regency vernacular once more. But then I realized that there was no way that Charlotte would know that it came from a gangster film in the future, and indeed she did not.

"Indeed," Charlotte echoed. "An offer that she cannot refuse."

I almost burst out laughing. However, I managed to suppress it and I only smiled giddily, but Charlotte noted that.

"Well, what is that smile for?"

"Oh, nothing, it is just, Charlotte, I do wish for you to know, that I do so much wish to find you with the good fortune of being happily married yourself."

"Well," Charlotte said, her eyes darting back and forth, unsure of why I would say that, "well, thank you, Lizzy, though I should be lucky if I have any of your good luck. Then again, I am not romantic as you know, and I merely ask for a comfortable home, yet you shall find it sooner than I."

"What are you talking about? We are both in the same place. Except that your father had sons to inherit his estate, making you luckier than I am."

"How so? How are we in the same place when Mr. Darcy is in love with you?"

When she said this, I quickly grew annoyed. Why was everyone seeing his attentions toward me as love and not only gratitude, which was all that it was?

"Charlotte, please do not misunderstand me, for I speak true. Mr. Darcy is just grateful to me that I saved his life and am open to his sister. Yes, he no longer finds me gruesome, and we are good friends now, but that is not enough for the foundations of a romance."

"Maybe towards you there is not, but for him, there is always that chance."

"Believe me, Charlotte; you do not know him that well. If he cared for me, he would have shown it by now."

"Perhaps he is only waiting."

"Waiting? For what, I wonder?"

"I am unaware. Only Mr. Darcy could tell you that. And don't you have to dance with him at this time?"

And only a minute later, Mr. Darcy had come to secure my hand for the set. As we went to the dance floor, and Charlotte was asked to dance by an officer, I smiled as I saw Mr. Bingley and Jane dancing with each other, and Georgiana standing up with one of Sir William Lucas's oldest sons.

"Your sister seems happy," I said.

"She is very happy. After all, Mr. Wickham is nowhere to be seen."

"He shall never come near her, I promise."

The music began and we both began to dance.

"You know of this?"

"I saw him again in Meryton."

I then told Mr. Darcy everything that had transpired between Mr. Wickham and me, and when I finished, Mr. Darcy ground his teeth.

"That worthless devil," he spat. "I wish to throttle him, truly. To accost you in such a vulgar manner and then try to spread his tale of lies. For I can assure you, Miss Elizabeth, that all he says are lies and no more."

"I believe you, therefore, you need not try and convince me. I put the truth forward, it made his cheeks redden and he was found out. Believe me when I tell you that Mr. Wickham will not come close to Georgiana at all. He is too much of a coward."

"Did you frighten him with your ferocity?" Mr. Darcy asked, smiling at me gently.

"Yes, I believe that I did. Now let us not talk of this, but something else, for we are at a dance. Let us be happy and enjoy ourselves."

"Yes, you are right. Please, tell me what you would like most to hear?"

"Well, we could talk about the number of couples in this dance, the size of the room, if private balls are better than public ones, but let us move past all the small mundane discussions of protocol and therefore proceed to other things. Besides Mr. Wickham, tell me about your childhood? Truly, were you a happy boy and was Georgiana a smiling baby?"

"Oh, we very much were happy as children, and then we reached our teens, which were a trying time for us both. Georgiana is still going through it, but she handles that age a lot better than I."

"Does she?"

"Yes, I was terrible when in my teens. I was so awkward, moody and fueled by sensibility rather than sense."

"You are describing all of us at that age, sir. And the truth is that you were normal. There were all the insecurities of that time, compiled with the change of body, mind and manner. We do indeed go from being a child one year to being considered full adults in the next. It is too soon a change, too drastic of one that I know. And let me see if I have this right, you were expected to grow up before you were ready?"

"Yes, that it precisely what it is. And as such, I feel this constant state of…"

"Hidden inadequacy?"

"Precisely! And yet it must always be masked by this decisive and determined manner. I never falter or break, because I know that I am not allowed to. Though in secret, I often feel like I am. How do you do this, Miss Elizabeth?"

"Do what?"

"Live every day with this intense pursuit of truth? Do you never find it exhausting?"

"Truth doesn't frighten me… as long as it is not scary."

Mr. Darcy smiled once more.

"Yes, well, I myself view the truth as the best and most virtuous thing."

"To the point where you choke others with it?" I joked.

"Yes, to the point of such."

"Well, we all forgive you!"

"Thank you, but I believe I have some news for you."

"Yes."

"Georgiana might be upset for me asking you first, but I wished to do so because I wished to convince you if you did not wish to go."

"What do I need convincing on?"

"Well, she was hoping to invite you to Pemberly."

"And you thought me willing to refuse that?" I laughed. "Mr. Darcy, have you so little faith in me?"

"I just wished to check. She wished for all of you to come, but I advised her against that, for we could not have Mary leave Longbourn just now, given her luck with your ghastly cousin. Dear lord, he is so obsequious. And we cannot deprive your parents of all their children, so it is best to leave Kitty and Lydia at home, though even their spirited wildness is also appearing somewhat charming in my eyes. Well, in Kitty's case, yes, but not so much in Lydia's. I mean not to offend you with that."

"No, I understand that she is full young, and I wish to improve her manner. Yet again, she is, as I said, young, and she might very well only need time."

"That is likely, yet we had settled to ask you and Jane if you would be willing to join us at Pemberly. For Mr. Bingley will also join us and therefore she and my friend can continue to improve the relationship that is developing between them."

"Oh, then that means that I must survive living under the same roof as Miss Bingley again. Well, no matter the ideal image, nothing can ever fully be perfect, and I suppose has no right to be."

"Oh, no, don't worry, for when we return to Pemberly, Miss Bingley and Mrs. Hurst shall remain in town, visiting with many friends."

"Then never mind, things can fully be perfect. Mr. Darcy, whenever your sister asks me, I am sure that Jane will accept, and I very much shall as well. Thank you so much for inviting us."

"And as much as I do not wish to shower you with much new news, but I believe this shall also be welcome. When we return, a cousin of mine shall break his journey there on his way to his home. He is in the army and his name is Colonel Fitzwilliam."

"Colonel Fitzwilliam?"

"Yes, he is the younger son to my uncle, the Earl of Matlock, and you shall like him. Indeed, he is one of my closest companions, and we always have been quite good comrades. He always has a way of making me lighter in manner, due to his lively disposition. And when we go into

Derbyshire, I can take you on trips to visit other houses in the area, and also to see the Peaks."

"You'll take us to the Peak District?" I gasped, happy to be going into Derbyshire again. "Really, oh but of course I would love to see it, and we shall be a merry gathering."

"Yes, I believe that we shall."

We danced on and, by the end of it, Jane danced three times with Mr. Bingley, making his attentions toward her quite clear. Mr. Collins danced twice with Mary, who for the first time admitted that she did enjoy dancing. Kitty and Lydia flirted the whole evening, my mother was overjoyed.

Mr. Bingley did not pay attention to any of her vulgar phrases and my father did nothing to check her. Georgiana allowed her bashfulness not to hold her back, Mr. Wickham was nowhere to be seen, and I breathed out a sigh of relief that all had gone well, and this was the ball to end all balls— for nothing unfortunate had occurred.

# Chapter Twenty

Naturally Jane agreed to go, and Mr. Bingley was glad of it. In a fortnight, we had packed and saw the departure of Mr. Collins back to Hunsford Parsonage, where he promised to return soon enough to further his courtship of Mary.

The officers sometimes visited our home, but it was only ever Denny, the Forsters, or Captain Carter, but never Mr. Wickham. Up until leaving for Derbyshire, I did not catch one glimpse of him, even in Meryton, which showed me that he in fact was willing to make himself scarce. All of which made me so glad.

By the end of a fortnight however, the time had come for us to leave for Pemberly. Our parents saw us off with happiness, for our mother expected Jane to return engaged, and me just to be me.

I embraced her and my father warmly before I left, for with my father, there was always witty affection, but with my mother, it was now something stronger than it once was. Kitty and Lydia were happy as always, and Mary, for the first time ever, looked complete and relaxed. Perhaps being tossed in love did do her some good in the end, and it gave her a sort of distinction among her companions.

"I am very glad that you are to join us at Pemberly," Georgiana said to Jane and me when we entered the carriage, "for the house shall seem so less lonely if you are there as company."

"Miss Darcy, we are very happy to be of service in matters such as friendship," I replied, and Jane echoed my sentiment. Thus, we departed with Georgiana, Mr. Darcy and the servant escort that Georgiana had when she rode to Netherfield initially. Mr. Bingley also joined us as the rest of the Netherfield party left for London. I was separated from Miss Bingley and Mrs. Hurst and now would be released from their scrutinizing eyes.

◈◈◈

Our journey had gone quite well, and safely we arrived in Derbyshire, and at last, we arrived at Pemberly.

It was precisely as I had remembered it from the exterior, and while I was speechless at it at first, Jane was profuse in her admiration.

"This is Pemberly!" she exclaimed. "Dear me, it so very beautiful."

"Yes, I know that Netherfield is nothing compared to it," Mr. Bingley admitted.

"Oh, nonsense, Mr. Bingley," Jane assured him. "For Netherfield is lovely, and also it is just as much about the company from within as it is from appearances without. And thus, you have quite filled Netherfield with your manners."

Mr. Bingley blushed at this.

"Very well said, Miss Bennet," Mr. Darcy complimented her.

"Thank you, Mr. Darcy."

"So, how do you like the house, Lizzy?" Georgiana asked.

"Oh, dear Georgiana, you need not even have to ask, for it is undeniable, that this is the greatest house that my eyes have ever seen. But I shall not be content until I have been able to go within it and see where you both grew up."

"Then inward we shall go."

The servants met us, along with the housekeeper, Mrs. Reynolds, and we entered Pemberly.

It was all the same!

Almost every room was quite similar to what I had first become acquainted with over two hundred years in the future. Yes, there was a different cushion here and there, but it was as if the family did everything to preserve the original look of the house. My heart warmed at the look of it, and I began to look at every wall, ceiling and room while forgetting myself and not paying attention to how I must have looked to the company.

Yet all the feelings began to rush back. Every happy memory that I possessed and coveted from when I had first come to Pemberly returned, for it was the first place I had felt at home when I had left Philadelphia. This was the first place I was able to fully rebuild my confidence.

Eventually I remembered myself, then turned to everyone else and they had looks of utter surprise on their faces.

"Oh, forgive me," I voiced. "It is just that... this is so... it is beyond what I could have expected."

"Then you like it?" Mr. Darcy asked.

I pressed my hands together and brought them to my chest. "Yes, I love it."

"And I love it almost as much as I love Netherfield," Jane said, smiling at Mr. Bingley, who blushed again.

⚜

Our first day at Pemberly was spent with us being given a grand tour of the house and then sitting down to a lovely dinner. The next day, we then were given a tour of the grounds and they were even more extensive than I remembered.

Yet on the third day, after breakfast, I told Jane to offer my excuses to Georgiana, for I wished to take a walk about the grounds alone for some time. I wished to enjoy the beauties of the grounds in peaceful solitude. In truth, this meant that I wished to run about the grass for a while, and I could not do it if I was in a company of others, as Jane very well knew.

Therefore, when alone on the grounds, I removed my bonnet and when I felt that there were no eyes upon me, I rushed along the grounds and began to enjoy the air around me. As I did so, I saw a dog dashing about, and I knew that the dog was Waterloo, and he belonged to Mr. Darcy. Therefore, as it raced along, I chased after it, then I grabbed a stick and began to make it fetch. As I did so, there was a rider across the grounds who I spied, and he rode close to me. I stood still with Waterloo next to me and the rider approached.

"Well," the man said, "I do believe that dog is Waterloo, and he belongs to my cousin Darcy."

In hearing the man mention Mr. Darcy, there was no need for alarm because it was clear who he was.

"Oh, then you must be Colonel Fitzwilliam!"

"I am indeed." He smiled, dismounting. "Now tell me, are you walking Waterloo, or is he walking you?"

"Neither, luckily. We are merely playing a lovely game of fetch the stick."

"I am going to assume that he does the fetching and you do the throwing."

"On the contrary, it is quite the reverse."

Colonel Fitzwilliam laughed at this.

"Well," I continued, "it is not so improper for us to become acquainted I believe. I am a guest of your cousins. My name is Elizabeth Bennet, and I am here with my sister, Jane. We are company for Miss Darcy. Also, in attendance is Mr. Charles Bingley."

"Yes, I was told of the merry gathering here." He bowed and his looks, while not the handsomest, had something still to recommend him. His smile was charming, his air was light and breezy, and his eyes were kind. Also, his form, from serving in the army, was somewhat muscular, but not overtly so. There was something about him that I immediately wished to like.

"Well, I am delighted to make your acquaintance, but I declare that I feel as if I know you already. For both of my cousins have written to me about you. And I do believe that I also owe you much."

"Do you? We have just met, therefore, how could you already be in my debt?"

"You saved my cousin's life," he replied simply. "Do not think, in the course of my life, that I shall ever forget that. In fact, I owe you much."

"You sound as if you are a man who feels deeply for his family."

"I do, and Darcy and I have practically grown up together. He's helped me more than I can say, and therefore I often do my best to return the compliment."

"A relationship where both sides equally depend on the other. My sister and I share the same situation."

"Refreshing, is it not? To have a bond such as this, especially in the times that we live in, where true emotion frightens all."

We walked together toward the house. "Precisely", I said. "We all talk nicely, but do not feel one emotion deeply, and call that logical. Oh, but there is a significant difference between logic and coldness. What about having a true feeling makes people almost die of fright?"

"I cannot tell you fact, but only an assumption that I have made just by observing the world around me. People fear feeling things, because they believe that if they feel one thing, then that means they should feel for everything. Also feeling things gives you something to lose."

I gave him a wry glance. "And people very much hate to lose."

"Yes, they do."

"Yet to this, I shall add one thing."

"And what is that?"

I took in a breath and began. "Feeling leads to people making mistakes. When you want something so badly, it is easier to do bad because it makes you nervous. Emotions, by their very definition, make us nervous. And whoever wants to play the fool? Whoever wants to be labelled as the idiot, the ridiculous one, or the one who speaks nonsense?

"The best conversations I have ever had are the ones where no one is afraid, and nothing is at stake. Yet when you care, it is easy to get tongue-tied; your words confused, jumbled and make a verbal mess of things."

"Precisely." He cocked his head in my direction. "Do you speak from experience or wisdom?"

"Experience is that word that we humans put to our past mistakes, and I have many of those. Therefore, if I am allowed, may I call my past mistakes as putting me on the path to wisdom?"

"You might as well, for that is what I do."

"Very well, then we are the same in another way, aren't we?"

"This bodes well for our future while remaining here, does it not?"

"Or poorly. For we have begun so high, and therefore how can we keep this up?" I said it lightly, keeping the mood as it was.

"I suppose we have to care, but also do our best not to let our emotions get involved, because if we do, then we shall grow to want to kick and punch each other out of the room."

I gave a merry laugh. "I think we have no fear of that, for we have just met. There's not enough room for us to do that."

"Time alone does not determine intimacy, I have found. Seven years can be enough time for two people to become acquainted, and for others, seven days can be more than enough."

"Or seven minutes in this case."

We both looked fondly at each other and then we burst out laughing.

"Dear me, how in the name of the holy book did we begin our acquaintance with such a conversation?"

He shook his head, still smiling. "I do not know, but I can assure you that I found it most amusing."

"I did as well. We make a wicked pair in that way."

"Yes, we do indeed, but I find that wickedness must always be forgiven in conversations, as long as it leads to wholesome actions."

"What wholesome action can we discover?"

"I do not know, therefore, it is best that you tell me."

Puzzled, I asked, "I tell you? You are placing all the responsibility on my shoulders?"

"A proper gentleman always asks the lady what she thinks. Then again, I am no proper gentleman. I'm a colonel."

"Well, whether you be a proper gentleman or proper colonel, it makes no difference to me. You still have placed the weight on my shoulders, and it was quite crafty. So much so that I applaud you for it."

"Oh, why thank you. So, what wholesome act do you proscribe to counteract our wicked tones?"

"Well, we are already doing it."

"Already doing it? What are we doing?"

I lifted the stick that was in my hand.

"We are playing fetch with a dog."

Colonel Fitzwilliam laughed as I threw the stick and Waterloo chased after it.

"Do you have a dog at Longbourn?" Colonel Fitzwilliam asked me as I escorted him to the stables. Waterloo trailed along next to us.

"No, we do not. We never have, for our mother did not like them. When we were children, we persuaded her to let us have two cats and they were brilliant. Unfortunately, one passed away when she was only five years old from reasons that we never learned and the other one lived to be seventeen and he died of old age, I suppose. After that, we were too devastated to own another animal. It was just too hard to lose them."

"I can well comprehend your feelings. I had two dogs growing up, and I still miss them."

"Were they hunting dogs?"

"Yes, they were. They were very affectionate. Amazing, is it not? That sometimes animals capture our hearts more than other people."

"Well, animals are constant. If you treat them well, they shall stay with you and love you. Unlike humans who can fall in and out of love so easily or betray you easily as well. We humans are rarely constant on anything, even when we ought to be. Therefore, dogs and cats, with their mindset, are purer than we are. They hold fast while we…"

"Break?"

"Yes, precisely. Thus, in some ways, they are better than we are."

"And all that we have to separate us from them is our rationality, reason and logic. But sometimes, it makes you wonder if having those things is worth it. Because we often use it, and then suffer in other ways. We often use it to make life so complicated."

The groom took his mount.

"Exactly what I have seen. Rules are needed because life must be regulated, but sometimes it is as if we make rules to restrict pure instinct and intention. We use reason to justify putting restrictions on the strangest things to do so, and therefore life can be quite suffocating. For example, my home, Longbourn, will not be inherited by me or my sisters, because it was entailed away to the male line. Therefore, my cousin, Mr. Collins, will inherit it. He, who never once lived in the house before."

"And of course, society calls it logical."

I gave him a quick glance. "Precisely. It placed a limitation on something that there was no need, and no logic to do in the first place. Rules are meant to regulate, not to smother one with."

"I have another complaint to add to this. Why, in our time, since so much importance is placed on wealth, it costs so much to live."

"Yes, so very true!"

"Yes, because our positions in society compel it. I am not the oldest, so I inherit little and therefore must have my profession, but the eldest gets most.

"Mind you, I admire having to work, but I should not be valued as being an insufficient man just because I do not have a large income."

"Just as I, as a woman, ought not to lose all importance in the world just because my father can only give me 100 pounds per annum."

"100 pounds per annum?" Colonel Fitzwilliam gasped. "Did your father not think of the future for his children?"

"Well that is his story," I replied, wondering why he was so taken aback by my confession when we were speaking of it a moment earlier.

"Yes, of course," Colonel Fitzwilliam replied, blinking and then returning to his traditional charming state. "Yes, I merely assumed, with you being friends with my dear cousin, Georgiana, that you were members of the ton."

"Well, I very much am not. I was born to Longbourn, which is where my estate is. My father is among the country gentry. We live comfortably, that is all."

I looked at him archly. "Well, are you going to find me inadequate for it, despite your declaration of otherwise?"

"Not at all," Colonel Fitzwilliam replied. "I just merely am amazed at you. You were brave, honest and proper to me from the beginning. I feel very much comfortable enough, and yes, we are similar again."

"Except that you can work for your fortune," I pointed out, "and I do so wish that we were allowed to as well."

"I could see you being a soldier," he joked.

"Yes, I do believe that I would look quite dashing in a red coat."

"Yes, Miss Bennet, I believe that you would have."

After delivering his horse to the stables we made our way to the house, with Waterloo next to us and Colonel Fitzwilliam scratching him behind the ears.

"Ah, he likes you," I noted.

"He likes you as well. Elizabeth Bennet; the girl who threw him a stick."

"Well, I have had many titles in my day, but that one is the most unique."

"I am happy that you like it."

We reached the house and entered it, where the company all assembled to meet the new arrival. When Mr. Darcy met his cousin, there was much affection between them. Colonel Fitzwilliam, between calling his cousin Fitz, being a little older in look, and clapping Mr. Darcy on the shoulder, very much was the older brother out of the two of them.

As we all sat down, Colonel Fitzwilliam was desirous to show his affection for Georgiana, and then wished to know all about Jane and me. We told him as much as we could about our lives, and to our surprise, he never was bored by it. When it came time for our meal, I had the good fortune to have had him seated beside me.

As he did so, he remarked on a story that Jane and I had told him earlier, about how we used to walk around as children on our tiptoes because we wanted to be taller.

"And how long did you all keep that practice going?" he asked in reply.

"In truth, we did not make for a full day, because our calves hurt too much."

"Well, if you think there is pressure on you for being a sufficient height, with us men, it is a necessity. If you are short, it makes you feel inadequate."

"Does it?" I asked.

"The world worships tall. Therefore, when I was blessed enough to have gotten to this height, I knew I was lucky."

"With us, irony rules our family. Our youngest sister is actually the tallest."

"Is she?"

"Yes."

"How many are you in number?"

"There are five of us."

"Oh, I should like to see you all together, for you must be a sight to behold."

"Something tells us that we are too much for one viewing," I responded with a wry smile.

"Well, I love looking at the image of things that I like again and again." His smile was charming. Amazed by him, I looked into his handsome eyes, he looked into mine and there was a moment that felt as if it had all stopped moving. His eyes were so warm and inviting, and I felt such ease in his presence.

Then I blushed and looked down.

"Do you like backgammon, Miss Elizabeth?"

"Yes, I do," I answered, gathering my wits.

"Is there any way that I can convince you to play me a set after dinner and when we gentlemen join you again? I have been longing to play a set."

"I am terrible at the game, therefore, you shall love to play it, for you are sure for success."

"As much as I hate to admit this, I do so sometimes like playing games where I am sure to win."

"You like to win?"

"Do not we all?"

I smiled once more and then I turned to see Mr. Darcy staring at us. I smiled at him, his eyes darted between his cousin and me and then he continued to eat his food.

Once the men joined us in the sitting room after dinner, Mr. Darcy sat near me quite quickly before Colonel Fitzwilliam could find his place on the seat nearby. But none of us thought anything of it, and so the Colonel sat down beside Georgiana and asked her about how her musical talents were progressing.

"I am still fond of music," Georgiana said, "and I wish to be progressing."

"Your cousin's musical talents confound us all and make us feel ever so inadequate," Jane replied. "I never had the talent to achieve a skill at music. Or, to be honest, I never had the patience or dedication for it either."

"Precisely," Mr. Bingley said. "There are so many things which I never mastered because I just didn't know how to bring myself to take the pains of practicing to aspire to such excellence."

"It is the hardest thing in the world," I said, "to sometimes push oneself in a direction one has no inclination to go, really."

"So, do any of you lovely Longbourn ladies play at all?" Colonel Fitzwilliam asked.

"Well," I pointed out, "I play and sing merely a little, but contain no perfection of any kind, or even mediocrity."

"I am sure that you are too modest."

"And to which you are, Miss Elizabeth," Mr. Darcy added, looking between Colonel Fitzwilliam and me. "For it is just as much about what one feels about what one plays as much as it is about their skill. Miss Elizabeth plays in so artless and sincere a manner that you feel that sincerity through the music."

I felt a blush creep up my neck. "Oh, this is so much praise, but the one time that you heard me play, Mr. Darcy, my mediocre attempts were quite saved by your lovely singing voice."

"You sang?" Colonel Fitzwilliam asked.

"Aye, he did it at Netherfield Park," Mr. Bingley confirmed. "And that quite shocked me, for many did not know that he could even sing."

"Yes, our families forced that lesson on us," Colonel Fitzwilliam added.

"You can sing as well, sir?" I asked.

"Oh yes, for the longest time, Darcy and I were forced to always sing duets."

Jane appeared surprised. "You were? Really. Two men singing duets? That sounds so lovely, and two cousins too. I declare that I have never seen such a thing."

"Well, if my cousin would be ever so willing, I believe that we could play for you now."

"Oh, Richard..." Mr. Darcy sighed.

"Oh, come on, Fitz," Georgiana said, "you both used to do it so often, and it's been so long since I've seen you two stand up together."

"And there's reason for it. Our families no longer forced us to do it."

"Oh, is there any way that we can persuade you both?" I asked innocently. "Please."

"I am for it," Colonel Fitzwilliam accepted, and Mr. Darcy scratched his chin and then sighed.

"Oh, very well. But only one song."

"One song is enough for me," I assured him. "It's just enough to look forward to."

Mr. Darcy stood up and walked over to the pianoforte as Colonel Fitzwilliam sat down to the pianoforte. Colonel Fitzwilliam chose the song, then he began to play and both men began to sing together.

As they did so, I left my seat and sat down near Georgiana, enthralled by the sight of them. There they both were, standing up with each other, both strong men of stature and appearance, and they were quite the sight. And the sound, for they had two strong and beautiful singing voices, and indeed, I felt quite put to shame.

"What do you think of them?" Georgiana asked me.

"I think that nothing is lovelier than the two of them as of now," I confessed. "And I never heard anything more delightful. It is quite infuriating how talented they are."

"I know your feeling. I never learned to sing that proficiently for I knew that I would never be as talented as they."

"I am sure that you are," I replied, still unable to take my eyes off the two men.

As they sang, Colonel Fitzwilliam winked at me, I smiled in return, and then I turned to look at Mr. Darcy, whose eyes were warm and gentle. By the end of their song, I could not tell who the lovelier man was.

Yet, like the rest, I clapped all the same and praised the talents of both. This time, however, Colonel Fitzwilliam was the one to accost me first, and then sit himself beside me.

"Do you know how talented you are?" I asked him good-naturedly.

"No," he replied. "I simply know how charming I am."

I swatted his arm playfully. "Oh, you're a cheeky one."

"I'm in the army. If there is one thing that we learn there, it is to be cheeky. And now, don't we have a game of backgammon to play?"

"Indeed, we do, and though I know that I shall lose the game, be prepared. I shall fight you until all of my strength is spent."

"There is nothing wrong with putting up a fight."

"Good, because a fight you shall have."

We removed the backgammon while the rest of the party played cards.

Mr. Darcy asked if I would join them, but I assured him that I was already occupied as the Colonel began to prepare the set. I did not know why he thought to ask me, due to the fact that I was clearly playing another sort of game, but so it was.

The Colonel laid out the pieces, I demanded to be the brown while he was playing the white and our game commenced.

"So," I began, "are you fortunate in that you are stationed very peacefully in Britain, or do you defend us against the French? Or even more unlucky, do you aid our forces against America?"

"Right now, I am stationed very peacefully here, but very soon I shall away to the continent and aid the resistance against our old enemy of France. Now, why did you say that fighting against America would be unlucky?"

"Because we lose, of course," I spoke before I could think, and then I bit my tongue in annoyance.

"You think we shall lose?" Colonel Fitzwilliam summed up. "And you speak it with such finality and conviction. So then, you really believe that we shall have no hope?"

"Well, it is not that I have any doubt of our strength. It is just my assumption from the little I know of the situation."

"And what do you know of the situation? What are your findings?"

"That we have to accept that we are a country going to war against a larger country across an entire ocean."

"Size alone does not determine victory. It's all about the fighting forces and strategy."

I moved my piece. "But right now, our navy is not at its highest powers. This is not the nautical certainty that we possessed in the Revolutionary War, but we are not that stable and fully aware of our powers. Our army is stretched thin between two fronts. Also, and I do not mean to offend you now, but King George is not the very best of rulers, and he has his father as a model before him that was not also the best in such matters. Literally, the sins of the father are now being repeated in the sins of the son: and that sin is blindness. They do not see the situation as it is."

"I do not deny that our leadership is not at its best, but in what way was it ever? We common folk shall always have some complaint to make of our royalty or political officials. And yet, it is a system that runs its occupants as much as they run it. Or even more so. Yet I know you to have a point."

As we played, we moved the game pieces throughout the board.

"Precisely, just because politics is quite cyclical does not mean that the same mistakes ought to be made. We must progress and move on. And while the idea of America returning to being our colonies is an interesting idea, the fact is that even if we were to win this war, it would only be a matter of time before they would revolt again and then would be victorious. The truth is that the only way a country of that size can remain our own, is if they choose it. I cannot help but feel so."

"That is the point, yet nothing is certain yet. We very well may win, or we very well may lose."

"Yes, you are quite right," I lied, "nothing is fully certain."

"But I applaud you on considering matters of the state and not limiting yourself on subjects that are labelled as being solely 'for the female mind'. I believe women are capable of much depth if allowed to bestow it."

"You are a man after my own heart!"

"I wish to believe so. But I should not be surprised; after all, I fight in an army, and you fight in the drawing room."

"And which circumstance do you think is more dangerous?"

"Oh, give me a battle and bayonet any day over the offensive measures performed in a sitting room."

I laughed at this.

"And I am honest and objective enough to know that is the safer choice."

"Yes, indeed it is."

"There is a greater chance for survival there."

Our conversation turned to witticisms and such lightness, that I was able to have him forget my bold declaration about Britain's eventual defeat in the War of 1812.

"So," I continued, "how long do you stay in Derbyshire, Colonel?"

"For almost a month in truth, and I am fortunate. I do so love this house."

"How can you not? But tell me, how does this house compare to your birthplace, Matlock?"

"Matlock shall always be home, but Pemberly is something else, you see. It is, well, it is hard to say, but Pemberly makes you feel as if…"

"Everything shall be well, and you are always safe."

He appeared pleased with my answer. "Well, yes, that is precisely what it is."

"And you cannot explain it, but it makes you feel such comfort, as if you need to be here always."

"Yes. Pemberly calls out to all of us, as you can see. It even brings out the best of my cousin, over there," he said referencing Mr. Darcy.

"Yes," I noted. "I have also seen how it brings out the most agreeable side of him. You both must care about each other so very much."

"Yes, we do. We are cousins, but a part of us does feel like brothers throughout this all."

"You give him company, and he gives you help, doesn't he?"

He slanted me a glance. "My goodness, you are a pertinent one."

"And I wanted to believe that you are the sort to not be offended by such frankness."

"Not at all. In fact, I find it quite refreshing."

"Do you?"

"Yes, indeed. As a man, I do not have all the time in the world that I would like, therefore life is too short to not always show what is inside of us, provided that it is not vulgar or base."

"Yes," I agreed. "In fact, when we were children, Jane and I had our moments when we were quite the troublemakers."

"Were you?" He gave me a playful smile.

"Yes, I loved to take off my shoes and wade in the streams, and I was quite determined."

"Oh, I still like to do that."

"And so do I," I rushed out. "I think it one of the most enjoyable of the smaller activities."

"Yes, it is. And there is a very small pond on the estate that is quite out of the common way."

I gave him a faux look of surprise. "Why, dear Colonel, are you a bad influence?"

"Ah, could you not tell? I am the very worst influence."

"Mr. Darcy loves you; therefore, you must be doing yourself a great disservice."

"A wicked trick sometimes, humility."

Eventually the night came to an end and I went to bed, happy to be at Pemberly, and to have made an acquaintance who I found immense pleasure with.

# Chapter Twenty-One

## THE PRICE OF A SECOND SON

The next day, I walked about the grounds, reading a letter sent to me from my mother, who wished to know all the details of how Jane was getting on with Mr. Bingley. Exasperated, I sighed, for we had only just come to Derbyshire but a little while ago.

Yet as I walked, I heard footsteps, looked up and smiled as I saw Colonel Fitzwilliam accosting me.

"I see that you are amidst a productive walk," I noticed.

"A good walk cannot help but make one content, and especially a walk throughout the grounds of one of the greatest estates in England. I have been making the tour of the park, as I generally do every time that I visit. Are you going much farther?"

"No, I should have turned in a moment. Yet I am very fond of walking."

"Then are you willing to take this way together?"

"With pleasure."

We turned and began to walk along the grounds.

"So, I have noticed that your sister and Mr. Bingley are quite taken with each other," he began. "Forgive me for being most direct."

"Yes, they are. They had the good fairy-tale fortune to have met at a ball and then fell in love soon afterwards."

"Meeting a great love of yours at a ball, well, that is what everyone only dreams about but never obtains. Your sister must be very special."

I kicked at a stone on the path and watched it skittle into the brush. "I believe so, and I am very happy for her."

"She does seem very well pleased with him. Bingley is a pleasant gentlemanlike man and he is a great friend of Darcy's."

"Oh! Yes. Mr. Darcy is uncommonly kind to Mr. Bingley and takes a prodigious deal of care of him."

He reached down and picked up a twig. "Care of him! Yes, I really believe Darcy *does* take care of him in those points where he most wants care. From something that he told me in our journey hither, I have reason to think Bingley very much indebted to him."

I gave him a brief glance. "And what is that?"

"Promise that you shall not speak of this to anyone."

"I shall not; you may take me into your confidence."

"It was Mr. Darcy that urged Mr. Bingley to reconsider not choosing your sister for a potential love."

"What did he tell you?" I asked, already knowing the information that he was about to narrate.

"Mr. Bingley loved your sister, but then between her societal limitations, his sisters pressuring him, and even Mr. Darcy's initial doubts on that score, there was a moment that Mr. Bingley was going to be persuaded that your sister was not a good match. Yet when Mr. Darcy came around and realized that your sister did care for his friend, Darcy began to support her suit in earnest and therefore encouraged Bingley to set aside any doubts and pursue her."

"Yes. In truth, Mr. Darcy already confided this all to me. I am happy that he changed his mind and allowed Mr. Bingley to choose his own mode of happiness."

"He did? My cousin must respect you a great deal, for him to bear his soul in that way."

"Now, let us talk of family. And your aunt is Lady Catherine de Bourgh of Rosings Park as well," I observed, for the subject had quite changed to our families.

"Yes, and every year, Darcy and I make a trip to visit her."

"How long is this visit?"

"Well, it all is up to my cousin, for I am always at his disposal. He arranges the business just as he pleases."

"And if not able to please himself in the arrangement, he has at least pleasure in the great power of choice. I do not know anybody who seems more to enjoy the power of doing what he likes than Mr. Darcy. For that I envy him a bit."

"He likes to have his own way very well," replied Colonel Fitzwilliam. "But so we all do. It is only that he has better means of having it than many others, because he is rich, and many others are poor. I speak feelingly. A younger son, you know, must be inured to self-denial and dependence."

"In my opinion, the younger son of an earl can know very little of either. Now seriously, what have you ever known of self-denial and dependence? When have you been prevented by want of money from going wherever you chose, or procuring anything you had a fancy for?"

He paused a moment, and then said, "These are home questions and perhaps I cannot say that I have experienced many hardships of that nature. But in matters of greater weight, I may suffer from want of money. Younger sons cannot marry where they like."

"Oh." I faltered and did not know why. "Can you not? But surely you have been given some sort of inheritance that should give you some comfort."

"Some, but not enough to be free to make all the choices that I desire. Therefore, all my life, it has been placed on me to not always marry of my initial choosing, as younger sons often can't."

"Unless where they like women of fortune, which I think they very often do."

"Our habits of expense make us too dependent, and there are not many in my rank of life who can afford to marry without some attention to money."

As he confessed this, I wondered if this was meant to be directed at me. Was he telling me this to put me on my guard and warn me that his flirtation was solely that and that I was not allowed to have any sort of hope on that score?

And yet...did I care? There was a feeling of unease within me, and I feared his words, and thus it was clear; I did care. Yet why did I care? To what level was it? And it became frustratingly clear to me that perhaps, so very quickly, I had begun to entertain feelings for Colonel Fitzwilliam.

Thus, I colored at the idea, then recovered, found my voice, and said in a lively tone, "And pray, what is the usual price of an earl's younger son? Unless the elder brother is very sickly, I suppose you would not ask above fifty-thousand pounds."

"Yes, fifty-thousand pounds would be ideal enough for the cost of a younger son."

"Then any woman of lesser fortune is rather unfortunate, is she not? Yet, never fear, Colonel, hopefully there is an heiress out there for you to find your happy ending."

He chuckled quietly. "Thank you, for you are very forbearing."

"I wish that I am. For if your nature is always this way, then you deserve her."

"Thank you."

We walked on a little in silence and I did nothing to fill it. It was clear that *that* door was closed off to me, and I did not know what to think on the subject.

"Of course," Colonel Fitzwilliam said out of nowhere, "nothing fully is certain. After all, I first must survive my service in the army, and if so, perhaps my standards will alter, my style of living and what is expected of me will be lessened and perhaps, I may marry where I choose."

"Perhaps your luck and living style will take that turn."

He tossed the twig beside the path. "Now then, all I would have to find was a woman who was content with simple ways of living," he noted, looking at me significantly.

"It all depends on her disposition, but mark me, Colonel, there is much a woman would undergo for the sake of the man she cared for. Do yourself more credit."

"And to the woman who I choose, perhaps I ought to give her more credit as well."

I raised my eyebrows and studied him. "Yes, perhaps you ought to."

Our mood lightened, and then we turned our conversation to more mundane and casual subjects.

# Chapter Twenty-Two

## THE GOOD NEWS

"S o," Colonel Fitzwilliam said as he convinced me to sit down with him in the music room, at the pianoforte, "I believe that you lie and that you can sing quite well."

A week had gone into his stay, and we spent a portion of every day getting better acquainted.

By that point, I knew his childhood stories, his teenage phobias, and his adult insecurities. In exchange, he learned of my childhood insecurities, my teenage phobias, and my adult stories. We were quite backwards in that way, but by the end of it, I felt as if I knew his spirit and soul through and through.

"Ah, you believe that I am stricken with false modesty."

He looked at me, amusement in his eyes. "I have never met with a woman who wasn't."

"Well, now you shall see an honest woman as opposed to one who is seeking a compliment."

"You shall play for me then?"

"Only to show you how abominable I am."

"Yes, well, my cousin plays perfectly. Every London woman of the ton plays perfectly. So, maybe the last thing I need here at this time is perfection."

"Well, if imperfection is what you seek, then I shall play for you," I said, flexing my fingers.

We sat down together, and Colonel Fitzwilliam chose a song that required a duet.

"Oh, so you are going to make me sing as well?"

"In for a pence, in for a pound."

"Very well, Colonel. Alas then, for here we go."

I began to play and away we sang. Overall, the Colonel's voice was much lovelier than mine. As we played, I felt his eyes upon me, smiling as he sang, and I felt the warmth from his company rest over me. After we had finished, I felt confident over the fact that I had not lost my way that much when we played, that he slowed down his singing to accommodate my slower playing, and we both felt very satisfied.

"There you see," I said, attempting to appear nonchalant. "Luckily you have the ladies of the ton with their large dowries and accomplished talents at music, or you would be forced to always be around my sort."

"You play very well," he offered.

"You flatter me."

"So?"

When he said this, I looked on him and his eyes were warm, and his countenance relaxed.

"I must confess," I said, "that I thank you when you do that."

"As you ought to feel, yet I do speak the truth and exaggerate in no fashion and…"

His expression shifted as he looked behind me and I turned to see Mr. Darcy.

I smiled when I saw him. "Mr. Darcy, did my voice annoy you so much that you had to come and tell me about it? Indeed," I stepped forward. "Not all of us can be as fortunate as your cousin and yourself by the way of singing."

Mr. Darcy did not reply initially and only stared me out of my countenance. Indeed, I did believe that he was angry with me, but I could not think of the reason why.

"Sir, is something of the matter?" I asked, a little insecure.

"Indeed, Darcy," Colonel Fitzwilliam spoke, "you look quite grave, man."

"Forgive me," he said at last. "But your sister Jane received a letter, and she claims that it is good news. Therefore, I came to fetch you to come to her."

"Oh, thank you, sir," I said, and then I came by his side. Colonel Fitzwilliam followed after me, but Mr. Darcy told him that he needed to do him a favor and go and check on his musket, because later on, he was thinking of them having a shooting party. Colonel Fitzwilliam gave me a pleasing look and then was off in a different direction.

As we walked, Mr. Darcy was silent and angry with me clearly, and I did not wish to waste time.

"Mr. Darcy, forgive me if I cause offense in any sort of way, but I must ask the question now, for fear that if we do not speak, we shall be the subject of miscommunication again, and I shall not allow that. Mr. Darcy, is there something wrong?"

"No, there is not." His voice was rather chill.

I stopped walking and turned to him.

"Mr. Darcy, what is it? No truly, I shall not walk further or let you do so, until you tell me."

When I spoke this, he halted, as I wished and then he began to wring his hands nervously.

"Well, you have been behaving..."

"Yes?"

"I have come upon you alone with my cousin."

"We were playing music. Even if that was lacking in propriety, then how could it be any less than Mr. Bingley visiting Jane in her bedroom at Netherfield when she was ill? Of course, those two had an understanding, but since there is none in the case of Colonel Fitzwilliam and me, what harm is there? Especially since he is your family, and I wish for them to like me."

"You wish for my family to like you?"

"Of course. Was that not the purpose of my coming? I wished to make Georgiana find me agreeable, and now a cousin of yours is on my hands, and I should really put my best foot forward in that respect. I thought... I am not making you happy in this way?"

"I did not know that was your intention. Yes, Miss Elizabeth, of course that is something I desired."

"Of course, I find your cousin most agreeable and everything charming, but that seems to be his special skill."

"You find him charming?"

"I am not blind, sir. And he is charming as you are sincere."

"Yes, you know my love for the truth."

I looked at him from beneath my lashes. "You were supposed to say thank you."

"Oh of course, thank you."

I laughed at this and Mr. Darcy appeared to relax.

"So, this is what you ask of me now? Are you sure this is all that was vexing you?"

"It is just that…"

"Yes?"

"We have not got that much of the chance to talk, as I had hoped when you came."

"You wished for us to get better acquainted?" I asked shyly. "But surely you know that is all entirely to your desire? If you wish for us to speak more, then for goodness sakes man, seek me out. Do not leave our conversations entirely up to chance. For Chance is a fickle friend. If you desire something, speak up and tell me about it. I can't know what you don't show me."

"I had not thought of that."

I shook my head and chuckled. "Come and sit down with me."

We sat on a bench that was in the hallway and I looked on him archly.

"What?" he asked.

"So, you do realize now that, sir, you preach one thing and then practice quite another."

Obviously confused, he asked, "Pardon?"

"You once chastised Jane because she did not show her feelings for Mr. Bingley, and then now you yourself barely show me anything when it comes to our friendship. Sir, are you now a hypocrite?"

"Well I…" he started and then he trailed off and rolled his eyes. "Oh, dear me, did I really just do that?"

"Yes, you did. And now that you have confessed it, it is most amusing, and I am not offended at all."

"You are not?"

"Of course not, for you realized what you did."

"Thank you."

"If it is of any consolation, even when you do such things, I shall always believe us to be friends, and I shall forgive you."

"Friends?" he echoed, questioningly. "Is that what we are?"

"Well, yes, come now, at least give me that, Mr. Darcy. Do you still not believe us to be that?"

"Well, I did not mean the reverse, of course not. Yes, I do quite like that you feel that way in regards to me."

"There you go, and if you like, you shall not lose me ever."

"I shall not?"

"No, nothing shall shake me."

"Elizabeth—"

He halted when he realized that he called me by my first name.

"Oh, forgive me."

"I took no offense, for you just feel so comfortable around me. And it's about time, sir!"

Mr. Darcy laughed at me.

"Now, you once complimented me on my fine eyes, so do me the favor of complimenting me on surviving you, because you do make it a trial sometimes."

"Very well, you survive me quite well."

"Thank you. Now then." I stood up and offered him my hands. "Come now, for we cannot keep my sister waiting, can we?"

Mr. Darcy took my hands and I pulled him up from his seat, much to his surprise. For a second, I grew quickly emotional when I recalled that I did that to his descendant once when we were seated at a bench behind Independence Hall. Yet I subdued the emotion and smiled. Sometimes I thought it ever so unfair that this Mr. Darcy was before me now, always reminding me of what Time had taken from me. For they looked so much alike and then for the one to look identical to the other... it only reminded me that I could not have something I sought after.

Yet was I blaming this Mr. Darcy now in some way for not being the other one? Was I not always seeing him for what he was because of a ghost, of a shadow that lingered over him, that he would always be unaware of? Was I being irresponsible somewhere? Yes, perhaps I was letting the memory of one not allow me to see the moments in the present properly, and this Mr. Darcy should not be blamed for that. Therefore, I supposed I only had to observe him closely to see how I was making him feel, because he kept some things quite hidden.

Ah, Time had things so very complicated.

❦

At last we arrived at the drawing room where Mr. Bingley was standing near Jane, appearing quite antsy. When seeing me, Jane jumped up eagerly, as if she were a spring in a box.

"Lizzy, it is the most wonderful of news!" she declared. "And I could not wait till you came because I could not speak about it until you had arrived."

"Yes, indeed," Mr. Bingley said. "She shall not even tell me. Miss Elizabeth, you really ought to read the letter, for I am dying to know about it."

"I promise, when she reads it," Jane assured him, "I shall conceal nothing from you."

Jane opened the letter and handed it to me, so I quickly began to read.

*Dear Jane and Eliza,*

*It is with great pleasure that I write to inform you that only a week ago, Mr. Collins returned to Longbourn and expressed his suit quite well, asking for my hand in marriage. He spoke his proposal with great decorum and honor, desiring a match between himself and our family, to yield the breach between us, and since I accepted with alacrity, not only have I done my duty to both my family, myself, and to the service of the church, yet also now it can be guaranteed that Longbourn shall always rest in the hands of the Bennets, and nevermore does our mother have to fear being cast out of our dear home. Indeed, she now calls me her beloved child, and I confess that the title does please me.*

*I hope to see my sisters return home for my wedding, which shall take place in a month's time. Our mother wishes to have many plans for the wedding, I keep on insisting that I need no such finery, but she is insistent. And I find myself willing to be treated in such a manner, for she very sincerely—in a touching way that I could not have foreseen— requested to be allowed to dote on me, and while you know that I care little for such frivolous nonsense, it does make her happy, and I found myself quite affected.*

*Yours etc.*

*Mary Bennet*

When I closed the letter, I couldn't contain my joy and I laughed gaily. "Our sister is to be married!"

"Really?" Georgiana asked. "Which one?"

"It is Mary." Jane smiled, happy to be finally able to tell them the news. "Our dear sister is now engaged to our cousin, Mr. William Collins."

"Oh, splendid then!" Mr. Bingley exclaimed. "And this means that Longbourn shall always remain in your family."

"Yes, and we are forearmed against the worst now."

"Ah, I see that I missed something," Colonel Fitzwilliam said as he entered. "Is there something fortunate that I must congratulate someone on?"

"Yes, it is the best of news!" I declared. "Our younger sister, Mary, has gotten engaged."

"Oh, splendid!"

"Yes, she has indeed," Jane confirmed, "and that is delightful, for it is a most eligible match—very good for our family. They are two people who have a similarity of temper and intention, which one ought to have when entering the married state. And who would have thought, that not only was Mary to be the one to save our family, Colonel, but she was the first one to get married? And to think, that always Lydia believed that she would be the first one to get married."

"Did she?" Mr. Bingley asked.

"Yes, and a part of me agreed with her, for the rest of us would just have to wait and see if our luck was only half so much."

"It might not be half," Mr. Bingley asked, "and perhaps, it might even be more so, if you wish it."

"Of course, I would wish it. Why would I not?"

Mr. Bingley looked torn at first, standing there very awkwardly, and then suddenly, he was stricken by a mood of courage and he turned to Mr. Darcy.

"Darcy, I know that I ought not to be so improper, but I must be bold and ask. Would you be willing to grant me the pleasure of speaking to Miss Bennet alone? Quite alone."

Jane looked at me and looked down as I turned to Mr. Darcy and he faltered.

"Well, Bingley, if…if…"

"Of course, he can," I said, taking charge as I grabbed Mr. Darcy's hand. This was quite presumptuous and improper of me, but I knew that our friendship could survive me being so forward, and that Colonel Fitzwilliam might even forgive me being so bold. "Miss Darcy, would you please grab your cousin's hand as we lead the gentlemen out for a stroll about the…hallway?"

Georgiana smiled, suppressing her laughter. "Yes, I quite agree."

She took Colonel Fitzwilliam's hand and we left the room, leaving Jane and Mr. Bingley alone.

We went into the music room, where Georgiana offered to play some music, and while she did it beautifully, our minds were distracted. As we sat there, Colonel Fitzwilliam looked at me from one side, and Mr. Darcy looked at me from another. And that was when I realized... could they both have fancied me?

No indeed, it could not be so. And yet, could it be? Yes, Mr. Darcy complimented me, but wasn't it simply gratitude, for I had saved his life? And Colonel Fitzwilliam flirted with me, but in the end, was it real? For he did need a woman of wealth—and yet he did say that he would be willing to adjust and change his life. Had I been blind? And if so, this would hurt someone in the end. No, please let it not be true, for if so, then I had taken a step too far.

Therefore, I kept my eyes ahead and focused on Georgiana as she played, not wishing to notice or care.

Eventually Mrs. Reynolds entered and informed us that Mr. Bingley and Jane wished for us to rejoin them in the drawing room. When we did, both shone with happiness.

"Well then?" I asked.

"Yes, well?" Mr. Darcy asked.

"I wish to inform all," Mr. Bingley said, smiling at Jane, "that ten minutes ago, I asked Miss Bennet to be my wife, she had the goodness to accept me and now we are very much engaged!"

The joy that was expressed all around could not be defined. I embraced Jane as she almost collapsed with happiness, Mr. Darcy clapped his friend on the shoulder, Colonel Fitzwilliam and Georgiana applauded and Georgiana also embraced Jane as if she was her own sister.

All the while, I avoided looking at Mr. Darcy and Colonel Fitzwilliam. It was something that I did not wish to face.

"I am very happy for you, Jane," I said.

"Yes, thank you, Lizzy," she replied. "Indeed, this is too much. Why cannot everyone be as happy as I am?"

"Because not everyone is you, and therefore not everyone can have your goodness."

"Oh, but if I could see you and Georgiana as happy. Would there was another set of men just for you."

"Well, I shall pray for it," Georgiana said.

"Yes, so shall I," I encouraged, "but if you would give me forty such men, I shall never be as happy as you. For till I have your goodness, I shall never have your happiness. Yet maybe, if I am very good, perhaps in time," I said, suppressing a laugh, "I shall be as lucky as Mary and have my own Mr. Collins."

"I doubt that your fortune should not be better," Colonel Fitzwilliam offered.

"Indeed," Mr. Darcy said, more grave. "Yes, you very much shall!"

I thanked them both, but then turned my attention back to Jane, willing to submerge myself into her good news rather than focusing on my confusing findings.

# Chapter Twenty-Three

## THE DISASTER

The next day, I walked along the grounds alone, for Georgiana had to remain inside, due to a headache upon her waking. I sat with her for a time, but when she fell asleep again, I left her alone, and walked about by myself, wishing for time to reflect.

To my surprise, as I walked, I heard a horse galloping and therefore I turned to see that it was Colonel Fitzwilliam, riding up on a stallion.

Yet let it not be said that I would ever let my feelings of unease for his emotional state lead to me shunning him in any way. He had always been kind to me, therefore, until the moment of disquiet came, I would never show anything else but merriment. Therefore, as he rode up, I rushed to him.

"Is that your horse again?"

He stroked the animal's broad neck. "Yes, indeed it is. It's the same one that I rode up from town, when we first met."

"It is beautiful," I replied, petting its nose as he slowed it down. "I do not recall giving it a compliment when I first saw it."

"I am glad that you like him."

"Yes, he is as handsome as Mr. Darcy's set."

"Do you like horses?"

"I was never much of a horsewoman sadly, but I can ride well enough. Walking is my great skill, and that is all."

"Well," he said, dismounting, "we really ought to find a way to change that. Until then, I was wondering if you would like to walk this way with me toward a pond on that side of the estate."

"Oh, why not, sir?"

He smiled and we began to walk the way, with me talking all the while.

Eventually we reached it. I began to walk around it, looking at it, when I saw Colonel Fitzwilliam sit down and began to remove his boots.

The sight of it made me laugh. "Whatever do you do, sir?"

"Seeing if you were willing to show me if the child you once were is still in that spirit of yours somewhere."

"Ah, is that what you do?"

"Come now, surely you can see that we offend and hurt no one, and the question then is, does Miss Elizabeth have spirit?"

"Yes, she does, but I do not wish to scandalize anyone who may look upon us."

He appeared downtrodden. "Ah, then you let me down. And here I thought that you were willing to be the bravest woman of my acquaintance."

"How dare you question my courage, sir?"

"Well, how can I not now?"

I rolled my eyes, then I leaned down, removing my shoes and stockings.

"Ah, and Miss Elizabeth has remembered herself!" Colonel Fitzwilliam declared as he offered me his hand, helped me up and we began to wade in the water together.

"Ah, is there any felicity in the world superior to this!" As we walked in, I said, "It is cold, refreshing and delightful."

"One time when I was on a ship, headed for the continent, the sailors all jumped into the water to swim around. At first, I was frightened, for it was such a large stretch of water, and I worried about what could be in it, but they assured me that they had swum in it often enough and nothing ever befell them. So, I gathered my courage and jumped in with them."

I pressed a hand to my chest. "You did that?"

"Yes, I did."

Very curious, I asked, "How did it feel?"

"Liberating. Out there, on the open sea, when no one sees you, you can find that liberty."

I gazed off into the distance. "I should like to have done that."

"As I suspected so. You seem so different."

"Different, how so?"

"You seem so free."

"Free? Well, I suppose that I do not like being shackled by things. Do not misunderstand me; I believe in decorum, propriety and sense. But in other things, I have learned, well, that there is not often anything to fear. The world is frightening, but I do not wish to be afraid of it anymore."

"Neither do I."

"I suppose, fighting in a war could do that to you."

"Yes, it does. Either, when fighting, and seeing men, well…"

"Die," I answered for him. "Do not be afraid to talk about it, Colonel. I am not afraid of the word."

"Thank you, well, when seeing men die, either two things happen: either you lose your humanity, or you cling to it. You crave for isolation for fear of harming others, or you desire human connection. You desire love."

"Both are perfectly natural reactions. Yes, they are."

We waded around a little longer. Then we had been gone long enough and it came time to return to the house.

We walked along in silence for some time and then we reached the stables. However, before we entered, Colonel Fitzwilliam stopped and turned to me.

"Forgive me," he began, "but we are quite alone now, and with the circumstance, I cannot help but feel as if I shall never get another opportunity."

I turned to him and waited, my heart pounding. What was he going to say?

"Miss Elizabeth," he replied, "when I said before that with us soldiers, our natures either seek isolation or love…"

"Yes?"

"Well, my character made its choice."

"And what was it?"

"Love. I seek love. And the truth is, that while for so long, I was expected to marry for fortune, in this moment, I cannot think so now. My heart feels this, and I cannot deny it. I do not know if it is because I am realizing that I do not have forever to wait or because of so many offers of marriage happening, but I shall not ignore my instincts anymore.

"Miss Elizabeth, in vain I have struggled, and it will not do. My feelings will not be repressed. You must allow me to tell you how ardently I admire and love you."

When he said this, I lost my breath, not knowing how to respond. Indeed, I felt as if the wind had been knocked out of me.

"And therefore," he continued, "I know I am not rich, have no chance of being so, but I believe that your nature, so open, so affable and strong, has the ability to live even through a small income. I believe that with you, love is enough. Therefore, if you would be ever so good, then I beg you to relieve my suffering and consent to be my wife."

As he said this, I was speechless still. My heart flailed against my ribs, seemingly intent on breaking them.

"Oh, Colonel...forgive this silence. It is just that I am so very surprised and feel as if you could knock me down with a feather."

"You could not tell that I was in love with you?"

"I did not tell myself you were, for I feared seeing something there where there was nothing."

"Well, now you see that there is nothing to fear. Now you see that I am sincere in my attentions. What say you, dearest Elizabeth? Will you marry me?"

For a second, I was hesitant, for I feared that my emotions were not as deep as his, until I realized that there was no chance for me in regards to my first love. And what I was feeling for the Colonel was enough for me to begin to feel again.

I just needed time. Time enough to see if I could feel fully, as I was already beginning to. Yes, we just needed a courtship, and I could very well see us getting along charmingly afterwards. Yes, maybe, I could see myself in another life than the one I had originally sought. It was time to relinquish any dreams elsewhere and find my place in the present. Therefore, I prepared to tell him that I wished to ask for a courtship, so he could determine if we were suited well for each other. But just as I smiled and began to open my mouth, I was shocked when I heard another voice.

"No, she must not!"

We both turned and rushing down the steps nearby was Mr. Darcy.

And that was when I wished to be any other place than where I was.

"Darcy, what the devil are you about?" Colonel Fitzwilliam shouted.

"Forgive me, Richard," he said, "the last thing I ever wish to do is harm you, but I cannot allow this."

"I know that our fortunes make us not that compatible, and I have not asked for her parents' consent, but I shall and..."

"I do not interrupt this meeting because of either of those things. Forgive me, Richard, but I cannot let you marry her. I cannot!"

"Darcy, I don't mean to hurt you either, but you really have no say in the matter, but—"

"I cannot have you marry her because I am in love with her!"

"What?" He nearly choked.

I closed my eyes, despising this very moment. How I prayed that it would have never come to this.

"Yes, I am, and I shall not let you propose to her, not when I wish to do it in turn."

At first, we were all quite frozen, just staring at each other. There is no way to get out of such a disaster, and one does not know whatever to do, and thus it became a larger catastrophe when Mr. Darcy turned to me.

"And before you argue with me, Richard, I believe that the question ought to be put to Miss Elizabeth now."

Both men turned to me and then I grew most vexed.

"Miss Elizabeth," Mr. Darcy said, "forgive me, but is there any gentleman whose attentions you prefer?"

"So that I can destroy your relationship?" I shouted, throwing up my hands. "So that I can say that I ruined a friendship between two devoted cousins? Is this what I am to be considered as?"

I stomped my foot firmly. "No, I shall not at this time, nor can I see myself ever doing it. I admire you both, but when it comes to love, I shall save you both by depriving you of what you seek. I shall not be the death of your camaraderie. No, I shall not, and I shall marry neither of you! Now excuse me!"

I walked quickly away, and then I heard some footsteps behind me.

"And if either of you follow me, I shall scold you with a fury," I declared. "And if either of you try and fight with the other, then I shall get even more irate and you shall never hear the end of it."

Therefore, I rushed away from them and into the house.

I raced to my room, collapsed on the bed and sobbed. How I wished that I had never come back into my own time! Yes, I was able to save Mr. Darcy, and encourage our mother to turn Mr. Collins's affections toward Mary rather than Jane, but I did not want this! I did not want to hurt either man, and would rather have faced heartbreak in the future than to break hearts in the present. All my efforts and this is where it had led me? I created discord between two great men, and now it was all to come to a crisis.

I suppose then that it was the price of Time being unwritten and then rewritten. For when it was so, then consequences had to occur in other places. I suppose this was that consequence, but I then realized that I was being quite selfish for wishing for the reverse. In coming back, Mary would marry our cousin, saving Longbourn, Jane's engagement to Mr. Bingley had come to fruition, and Mr. Darcy was alive. Therefore, my temporary discomfort was the price, and it was a little one. Therefore, I had no selfless reason to lament.

# Chapter Twenty-Four

## THE FAMILIAR FACE

A nd at present, both men proposing at once led to me being quite faultless. They could not blame me, or I with them. I made the only choice that could be made, and thus at least I was satisfied in that way. I could not be thrown out of Pemberly, because I was the one who was placed in the horrible position. Therefore, there was nowhere else for me to go, and that was good enough for my peace of mind.

Yet as I sat there, the minutes ticked away and yet a stomachache—the one that comes from feeling such unease and nerves—came to me, and I did not want to leave the room. No, it was too much, and I did not wish to be released from the safety of my room. Yet when two hours had come and gone, there was a knock on my door, and it was quite hurried.

"Lizzy?" Jane cried. "There has been a calamity!"

"A calamity!" I echoed, and then I rolled my eyes. Indeed, with all that had been occurring, now there was another crisis!

Why, when all felt as if it was coming undone, this was to add to the pot of misfortunes. Well, I could not remain and act weak, therefore, I stood up, rubbed my face, threw away all selfish feelings of disappointment and opened the door.

"Jane," I began, "what is it?"

"It's Mr. Darcy. He's fallen."

"Fallen," I gasped, afraid of any and every implication that the word gave. "What do you mean? Is he alright?"

"Well, he is fine in body, but his mind is disturbed. And his clothes also are a curious thing, for I have never seen anything like it, well, except for that time you came to Longbourn and were wearing the strangest attire."

When Jane said this, I immediately turned cold at the implications.

"Jane, what do you mean? What happened?"

"Well, you must come, for he is calling for you."

"Very well," I said, and I followed after her quickly.

"It is the strangest thing. For he looks at his sister and Mr. Bingley as if he didn't know them, but he said that he was seeking after you, and recalls you with perfect clarity."

"Jane, tell me, is he soaked? As if he was swimming?"

"Yes," she replied, eyeing me shrewdly. "Yes, he must've been riding by the pond on the outer parts of his estate. But his clothing…"

"Yes, yes, yes!" I muttered and then I began to pull her along, forcing her to run. "Just take me to him quickly."

We raced along the hallways and then eventually we came into the drawing room where first we were met by Mrs. Reynolds, who turned to me with pleading eyes. I walked past her and then saw Mr. Bingley and Georgiana looking at a man sitting there, and their faces were quite bewildered.

I moved around them, and sitting there, I was met with the familiar face. Despite looking exactly like his ancestor, I knew him immediately, for nothing could deny that he was wearing the same jeans, Stretch-T, blazer and overcoat that he had when last I saw him. When his eyes rested on me, he sighed out in familiarity and happiness.

"Elizabeth!"

"Mr. Darcy!"

There, before us all, was Mr. Fitzwilliam Darcy…from 2016.

Don't miss out on your next favorite book!

Join the Satin Romance mailing list
www.satinromance.com/mail.html

# THANK YOU FOR READING

Did you enjoy this book?

We invite you to leave a review at your favorite book site, such as Goodreads, Amazon, Barnes & Noble, etc.

## DID YOU KNOW THAT LEAVING A REVIEW...

- Helps other readers find books they may enjoy.
- Gives you a chance to let your voice be heard.
- Gives authors recognition for their hard work.
- Doesn't have to be long. A sentence or two about why you liked the book will do.

# About the Author

**Ney Mitch** has been a long-standing Jane Austen enthusiast, having written forty novels that were inspired by her various works. Since stumbling on Miss Austen's books after graduating from college, she has always dabbled in Austen inspired literature, ranging from writing works for teens to adults. Originally, her desire was to adapt Jane Austen's writing in a way to help young adults connect with her, however over time, she has spread her aims to other genres and styles.

Having received her BA Degree at Desales University, she is a writer, both literary and dramatic, as well as being a Historic Reenactor.

 facebook.com/courtney.mitchell.589

 twitter.com/CMMitchelPsyche

pinterest.com/shebaanna

# Also by Ney Mitch

WITH SATIN ROMANCE

### *The Memory Series*

Moments of Moments Past

❦

### *Pride & Prejudice Reimaginings*

Rapture & Rebellion

www.ingramcontent.com/pod-product-compliance
Lightning Source LLC
Chambersburg PA
CBHW020439180626
46812CB00003B/1316